BLOOD MARKED

StarHaven Sanctuary: Book Three

Tera Lyn Cortez

DEDICATION

For my readers and friends who have stuck by me through the stress of the last year and a half and waited ever so patiently for this trilogy to finally be completed! I appreciate you all!

CHAPTER ONE

The chair legs crashed against the table as my knees gave out and my butt slammed down into the seat. Blinking rapidly, I attempted to clear my vision, praying that the shards of glass littering the tabletop would rearrange themselves somehow, reforming the vessel I'd (somewhat arrogantly) believed to be unbreakable.

Please, please, please let this be some sort of terrible daydream. Maybe I'd drifted off at the gravesides and none of this was real. Pinching my forearm I begged myself to wake up. My state of mind remained the same, and all I had to show for it was a big ol' bruise forming.

Thoughts of the man I'd seen standing in my kitchen mere seconds before ran through my mind. His face seemed vaguely familiar, yet at the moment my panic prevented me from placing him. Did I *really* see fangs? Or is my imagination playing tricks on me? It had to be my imagination. There was no such thing as vampires. More proof that all of this was just a dream.

Of course, not that long ago I didn't believe there were witches or werewolves in our world either. The rude awakening I'd received should have opened my mind more fully to the unexpected. To the many things existing right in front of our faces, hiding in plain sight. Once again, frustration at being raised completely in the dark bubbled to the surface. I wondered if having the background knowledge would have left me in a better position to defend those I loved. If my mother had embraced who and what she was, she might not be dead now.

Then again, Aimee had spent her entire life with all the knowledge and ability to nurture her magic and still lost the battle. A wave of grief slammed into me. If I hadn't already been sitting in the chair, I'd have found myself on the floor.

The three of us together, though? What a team we would have made. We would have been able to beat her. Of that I had no doubt. I'd captured her once. I just needed to figure out how to do it again, and this next time I wouldn't let my guard down and allow her to be freed.

Vibrations rumbled as Rick and Isaiah came thundering up onto the back porch. I'd been so lost in my grief I hadn't felt them drawing nearer. They both stared at me with expectant expressions. Words failing me, I gestured vaguely toward the mess on the tabletop.

"Is that what I think it is?" Rick's eyebrows touched his hairline.

All I could do was nod.

"What in heaven's name happened?" Isaiah glanced sideways toward Rick.

Wiping my face on my sleeve, I sucked in a deep breath. "I went out to sit by Mom and Aimee's graves. I left the vessel sitting on the table here, because I felt like it would be disrespectful to carry the one who had murdered them to their graveside. I didn't want to offend their memory, and I kind of didn't want her to be able to gloat that she killed them, if that makes sense?"

Covering my face with my hands I let out a shuddering sigh. The men murmured their understanding and waited patiently for me to continue, not asking questions or rushing me. With a sniffle, I put my hands down and looked over at them, guilt choking me.

"I was just sitting there when I heard glass shatter. It was so loud, I originally thought it might be a broken window or something. I ran back in here as fast as I could. I got through the door just in time to see some guy standing here over the broken jar."

"Someone was in the house? That shouldn't be possible." Rick looked around the room, as if expecting to see someone else still there.

Both of them inhaled deeply. Rick closed his eyes and Isaiah looked around the room. Neither of them seemed satisfied with whatever they had been looking for.

"He looked vaguely familiar, but I was so busy panicking that I couldn't place him at the moment. And he left the second I got back into the house. So fast. Like a blur. His face is burned into my memory now, though."

"You think it's someone from one of the packs?"

Isaiah managed to look both worried and angry at the same time.

"You guys might think I've lost my mind, but..."

For a second, I didn't want to admit that I thought I'd seen a man with fangs in my kitchen. They might think that the stress finally broke me. At this point, I didn't know if I could handle them thinking that I'd lost my mind.

"Yes?" They both wore identical expressions of concern and confusion.

Inhaling deeply, I took a second to try and frame the sentence in the least insane way possible. "So, he grinned at me before rushing through the house and out the front door. I could have sworn he had fangs. Like real, honest to goodness, sharp teeth."

Waiting for them to laugh, I kept my eyes trained on the tabletop.

"That's not possible." Rick was the first to speak.

Torn between wanting to defend myself and avoid the rest of the conversation altogether, I snorted. Even having expected this reaction from them, it still hurt. Before I could argue, Isaiah chimed in.

"The stories are true. Vampires cannot enter without being expressly invited. With the extra wards on this house, I don't see any way he could have gotten over the threshold."

His response left me momentarily speechless. They didn't think I was crazy. In fact, they didn't even question my assessment of the man's teeth. Instead, they were astounded that a vampire could have weaseled its way into the house.

"We need to figure out where you have seen him before. I can't imagine Aimee would have ever invited one of them into the house." Rick looked towards Isaiah.

"And your mother most likely knew better, even if she never would have admitted it."

Something wiggled in my memories when he mentioned my mother. The visitors from a while back, the ones claiming to be officers... Could that be where I had seen this man before?

"I think this was my fault." I sighed, hiding my face once more.

"What do you mean?" Isaiah reached out and gently pulled my hands away from my face. "Talk to us, Leah. We can't fix what we don't know."

"So, a while back, two men came to the door, claiming they were police officers who wanted to discuss Aimee's death. I told them to come in while I found my mother to join us. She came racing down the hallway and basically slammed the door in their faces after yelling to them that they were most certainly not welcome here. After that, she yelled at me for inviting total strangers into the house, and didn't I know how dangerous that was?"

The situation made sense now, but at the time, I'd been baffled by her reaction. I'd never seen her be so totally rude to visitors in my life. She hadn't bothered to explain the reasoning to me then, and once more left me to figure things out in the heat of the moment.

"She tried to take back my invitation to come in by telling them they weren't welcome here, but maybe it was already too late? They didn't even argue, just smiled politely and turned around to leave."

Rick nodded. "You had already extended the invitation. You would have had to be the one to take it back, for lack of a better term, in order for it to stop them, and even then, if they are strong enough, you wouldn't be able to reverse it."

"All they needed to do after that was bide their time." Isaiah frowned.

Cradling my head, I dug my fingers into my forehead and my thumbs into my temples, rubbing in circles. How could I have been so stupid? The building headache forced my eyes closed for a minute. Deep, even breaths helped me to gain control against the rising hysteria I felt burbling up inside.

Opening my eyes, I looked at the two men. "How can I stop them from coming back? Can we do anything to prevent them from being able to just show up and come in any time they want to?"

Rick nodded. "Yes. There is a ritual you can perform. You'll want to do it downstairs in Aimee's special room. You'll need to ask the goddess to grant her protection over the home once more, and ask her to rescind the validity of the invitation."

"Okay, I can do that. I'm going downstairs to do it right now."

In my attempt to push the chair back from the table, I somehow managed to tip it on the back legs instead of sliding it across the floor. The sudden shift in balance caught me off guard. Arms and legs akimbo, I crashed backward, slamming my head into the floor. Closing my eyes against the sudden array of stars dancing in front of them, I sighed until my lungs emptied of breath.

Isaiah took my arm. "Are you hurt?"

Not wanting to speak just yet, I shook my head. This whole being clumsy shtick was really beginning to get on my nerves. Despite being less than graceful my entire life, I'd felt even more like a klutz since arriving at the sanctuary. My own feet seemed out to get me. It surprised me that so far I hadn't wound up with more serious injuries.

"Ready to get up?"

At my nod, Isaiah gave my arm a gentle pull, helping me into a sitting position and shifting me off the uncomfortable wooden chair. Cautiously, I opened my eyes, shutting them again when the room spun out of control. Even with my eyes closed, I knew Rick had moved around to my opposite side.

"Take it easy. There's no rush. You might have given yourself a concussion."

When the mere act of shaking my head made me nauseous, I had to admit, at least to myself, that he might not be wrong. I opened my eyelids just a crack, giving me a view of my own legs and the floor. After blinking a couple of times I chanced opening them the rest of the way. With a few more blinks, the blurry vision cleared, mostly, and I looked toward Rick.

"Nah. I think I just need a minute."

"Mm. Denying it won't make it go away."

"I need to get downstairs and perform that ritual. The sooner the better."

Isaiah interrupted me. "You need to rest for at least a little while. How are you going to channel powerful magic from the goddess herself if you are so disoriented you can't even stand?"

Refusing to sigh again, I held my breath. Rick chuckled.

"You need to breathe. The last thing you need is to pass out and hit your head again."

"Oh, for crying out loud. You're not wrong. Can I at least rest somewhere other than the kitchen floor?"

Rick took my other arm. "Let us help you to the couch. Please don't argue. Consider it humoring an old man if you don't want to admit to yourself that you need the help."

The image of him as an old man elicited a small grin, and I agreed. "Fine, old man. Who am I to argue with that?"

The act of getting to my feet made me wince, even with their help. The chair back had created tender spots from my shoulders down to my hips. It made me grateful they had suggested the living room, where the couch was at least cushioned.

The trek to the couch wound up feeling about three times as long as it normally would. Every step made my hips ache. By the time they helped me lower myself onto the couch, the dizziness returned and I had to close my eyes to keep from vomiting.

Isaiah grabbed a pillow and situated it under my head to let me relax completely. Reaching out, I squeezed his forearm in thanks, semi-afraid to speak in case I got sick when I opened my mouth.

"I want you to rest so you can regain your strength and be ready to do the ritual before dark. Isaiah and I will start deciding what we need to do next."

Before I could even open my mouth to protest, Isaiah put his finger against my lips. "Don't argue. We'll just be in the kitchen. We won't actually do anything without talking to you, we promise."

"Okay." I whispered the single word and decided to follow their recommendations. Whether I wanted to admit it or not, I couldn't do anything productive in my current state.

Sleep must have overtaken me, and the next thing I knew, I heard Isaiah shouting my name. It jerked me awake, causing me to sit straight up and my head to spin again.

"Huh? What?"

He and Rick entered the living room side by side. "I think we have some unwelcome guests. We need you to get downstairs and perform the ritual *now*."

The urgency in his voice drove me to my feet. The room tilted sideways. They caught me just in time to keep me upright.

"Help me. I'll never make it down the stairs on my own."

They half carried me to the secret room. Rick had to hold me up as Isaiah removed my shoes and socks. Between the two of them, they managed to settle me onto the earthen floor without letting me hurt myself any further.

As I dug my toes into the loamy warmth, the men stepped backwards, closing the door and leaving me in privacy to do what I needed to do. Before beginning, I took three deep, cleansing breaths. We desperately needed this to work. At this point, a battle with the vampires would cost us dearly.

"Hear my pleas, Goddess. We ask for your intervention, for your protection and for your blessing..."

CHAPTER TWO

A rumble shook the house as the ground rippled beneath me. My pleas increased in intensity as I begged for her to spare us and give us an opportunity to prepare for this new onslaught from the vampires and whoever they were working with. In exchange for her protection, I promised to rid her sanctuary of the evil within it.

"I will not let them sully your beautiful sanctuary. We will run them out and never let them return."

The earth heaved once more, as if releasing a big

sigh, and everything stopped. Isaiah called my name from outside the heavy wooden door. At my reply, he opened it, peering in expectantly. Heaven only knows what he thought he might see, but he looked markedly relieved to find me sitting exactly where they'd left me.

"You did it!"

"She did it." I held out my hands. "Help me up, please?"

He lifted me to my feet, and I immediately stumbled, causing him to catch my arm. "Let me help you get back up to the couch. Unless I can convince you to go to bed for a little while?"

"Nope." I started to shake my head, but stopped when it made me dizzy. "I will rest, but we don't know how much time we really have. Or if the rest of the pack is protected. What happened anyways?"

Rick rubbed his forehead. "We started to see shadows just outside the clearing. At first it was one, maybe two. We weren't sure if our eyes were playing tricks on us or not. Then a couple more showed up, and we became positive. It seemed like they were looking for a way to get into the clearing. When the first one made it through was when we knew we couldn't wait any longer and woke you up."

"We are ill-equipped to have a fight with a single vampire at the moment, much less a group of them." Isaiah's hand tightened on my arm as I stumbled in my weariness.

"You've got that right. I don't feel like I could win a fight with a stuffed kitten."

The interminable walk back to the couch finally ended, and I sank into it. Despite the fact that all I had really done was beg the goddess with my voice, I felt as if every ounce of strength I possessed drained from me during the process. Just holding my head up off my chest required immense effort, so I let it fall back onto the couch, leaving my eyes closed.

"You rest. You are not going to be much help with anything until you regain your strength."

"Ouch. No help with anything, huh?"

Rick laughed as Isaiah attempted to correct himself, then gave up. "Just get some sleep, okay? We know we have at least a little time and for you, it would best be spent regaining your abilities. You know, like to walk on your own and maybe-"

Mustering up the last of my energy, I threw the throw pillow at his head. It may not have had much oomph behind it, but it hit him square in the face. Rick's chuckles evolved into full on laughter as he warned Isaiah to give up.

"Just leave her to rest, son. When the hole gets too deep, you should just stop digging."

Giving him a half smile, I waved my thanks as I drifted off to sleep. My ears registered Isaiah still trying to talk to me, but I made no effort to stay awake and hear what he had to say. The exhaustion put everything into sleep mode whether I wanted it or not.

By the time my eyes opened again, darkness had settled in the room and left it shrouded in shadows. For a brief moment I panicked before realizing where I was. In the other room, I could hear Rick and Isaiah talking with at least two other people. I needed to freshen up before seeing anyone else. So, with exaggerated caution, I swung my legs over the edge of the couch, concerned about whether they would hold me.

In the end, their strength wasn't the issue. Someone had covered me in a blanket. That giant square of cushion-y warmth became entangled with my limbs and I didn't even realize it until I tried to take a step. All my effort won me was to find myself pitching forward, arms pinwheeling as I landed (loudly) on the coffee table.

The resounding crash brought not only Rick and Isaiah, but the previously heard visitors running into the living room. One of them flipped on the lights. Blinking at the sudden onslaught of brightness, I peered up at them.

"What on earth happened?"

"Are you okay?"

"Who the hell did this?" I gestured toward the blanket still wrapped about my legs.

Rick raised his hands in innocence while Isaiah once more attempted to explain himself. "I wanted to make sure you were sleeping comfortably."

"Can you please help me up?" I studiously ignored the other two people standing there, witnessing my embarrassment.

"Careful, there might be broken glass." Isaiah gently lifted me to my feet, setting me out of the way of anything that might have broken when I crashed down onto the table.

Rick held out his arm for support as I unwound the blanket. "Do you feel steady enough to walk?"

"YES! I would have been fine if not for this deathtrap." I gave it a disgusted glare as I threw it onto the back of the couch. "Sorry. Not your fault. I don't mean to be rude."

He just smiled. "It's okay. Why don't you go freshen up? We, and by we I mean Isaiah, will get this mess cleaned up and we will meet you in the kitchen whenever you're ready."

Isaiah's grumbling voice followed me as I stalked down the hallway toward the bathroom, but I paid him no mind. Despite knowing in my head that none of this could be blamed on him-seriously, he wanted me to be warm and comfortable, it's not his fault I have zero grace-I just wanted to be cranky and felt it best to ignore everybody until I got over it.

Shutting the door to the bathroom behind me, I leaned against it and slid down to sit on the floor. The nap should have helped me feel less sleepy, but my body insisted I could sleep for a week. At least. Stripping off what clothes I could while sitting, I crawled into the shower stall and turned the water on. Kicking off my pants, I pulled my legs in and let the warm water sluice down over my achy body.

As my skin adjusted to the temperature, I kept turning the handle for hotter and hotter water until turning it any more was impossible. Waiting until the water ran cold, I stood there, just trying to regroup.

Turning off the water and grabbing a towel, I resigned myself to having to join the others in the kitchen, whether my mental state was ready or not.

Realizing I hadn't grabbed clean clothes, I sighed, reaching for the pants I had carelessly kicked off earlier. The pants that had landed in the toilet bowl and spent my entire shower soaking up the cold toilet water. Fuck.

Throwing them down onto the shower floor, I pulled on the dirty shirt and wrapped my towel around my bottom half. Only a few doors down the hallway separated me from my room, where I could find clean, dry clothes to put on. Surely I could make it halfway down the hallway without incident, right?

Right. Success was mine. However small, I celebrated with a little jig as I reached for something clean to put on. And stubbed my toe on the leg of the dresser. Which caused me to knock my very-unfunny bone as I reached down to rub the offending digit. I cussed. Loudly.

The temptation to slink back down into the basement and curl up in the warm dirt of the sanctuary room almost overwhelmed me. Before I'd even gotten all my dry clothes on, a knock sounded on the bedroom door. Isaiah's voice followed.

"Are you okay in there?"

"Yep. Just stubbed my toe. Almost ready," I called out with as much fake enthusiasm as I could muster.

"Are you sure?"

"I'm fine!" Despite my resolve to not snap at him, that is exactly what I did, making me feel guilty again. "I'm sorry, Isaiah."

No response. I walked over to the door and cracked it open. The hallway was empty. Damn it. Now I had offended him, and he left. Not that I blamed him. I'd be getting tired of me and my attitude too.

With a sigh, I grabbed a rubber band to pull my hair into a messy bun and left the room. Making amends was more important than doing my face up. Hushed conversation filled the kitchen.

Rick looked over at me as I walked in. Isaiah ignored me. Shelby and a man I didn't recognize sat in the other two chairs. Shelby jumped up to give me a hug. Her arms wrapped around me and squeezed. It felt good, and I returned the gesture.

"How are you doing?" She looked into my eyes, and I could feel her concern as she studied me.

"I'll survive. It'll have to do for now. What's going on?"

Shelby gestured to the man accompanying her. "This is David. He has noticed some strange things going on that he felt like Rick and Isaiah ought to know."

Seating ourselves back at the table, I looked around it expectantly, waiting for someone to fill me in. Isaiah ignored my gaze by studying the trees out the window. Rick took a deep breath and began.

"Some of the pack has gone missing. They're just gone. Not a word to anyone else and there has been no trail left behind for anyone to track them. It's like they disappeared into thin air."

Pinching the bridge of my nose, I tried to figure out a way to word my question that the newcomer would not find offensive. "Do you think they disappeared willingly?" That was the best I could do.

He shook his head. "Nope. Not at all. All but two of them have a family, with children at home. They're not just running off on their own. Something has to have happened to them. These are men and women that are loyal to the pack, and always have been."

Isaiah spoke up without meeting my eyes. "Many of them are people I have known my entire life. And before you argue, I am aware that people change and that it is possible for people to be swayed by outside influences.

While I might buy that one or two of them were persuaded to join the outsiders, not all of them."

Rick agreed. "Too many have disappeared for me to believe they all defected to the other side. Plus, it's happened way too quickly."

Their insinuation about how many people we'd lost scared me. "How many?" I almost didn't want the answer.

You could tell Rick didn't really want to give it to me, either. "Nine."

"Nine?" I yelped the number in response.

After the number we had lost in battle, having that many of the pack disappear came out to an uncomfortable percentage of the total sanctuary population. Whatever was happening, we couldn't let it continue.

"What can we do? Is here anything I can do to help? Do you think having asked for the goddess's blessing will protect them now?"

"I don't know." Rick's head hung, and his chin hit his chest.

Isaiah sat staring silently out the window, and I could feel the weight of the responsibility on his shoulders, making me feel even more guilty for being a brat to him. These people were not just members of his pack. They were his friends and family. They meant something to him, and he felt responsible for their safety. Knowing him, he held all the guilt on his shoulders.

Under the table, I reached out and put my hand on his thigh, squeezing gently. Words didn't seem appropriate, but I wanted him to know that I would be there for him no matter what. Attitude or not, I needed to be more supportive of him. None of the blame for what had happened belonged to him.

For a moment he sat still, muscles tense, and did not acknowledge me. In the end, he relaxed, and I felt his hand cover mine. Letting out my breath, I thanked the goddess silently that he forgave me. What would I do if I drove him away?

CHAPTER THREE

"There's one other thing, as much as I hate to mention it. Aaron has gone missing too. I'm not sure if he has been subjected to whatever is causing the others to disappear or if he is involved." David looked uncomfortable at having to bring it up.

"We exorcised the evil spirit from him. I can't see him as doing those kinds of things without her influence." Rick seemed fairly sure of himself.

"Did we get her completely out, though? What if she still had some control over him, even though she no longer occupied his body? Like a residual stain that wouldn't completely go away?" Isaiah seemed just as sure as Rick, but for the opposite possibility.

"I have to admit that we can't afford to rule anything out at the moment. I was absolutely certain that she wouldn't be able to escape that vessel until we chose to allow it, for whatever permanent solution we came up with, and here we are. The outsiders who she is involved with must have some pretty powerful magic of their own."

My stomach churned at the thought that I had inadvertently led us into an even more dangerous situation by leaving the vessel that contained my grandmother's spirit unattended. If it had been in my pocket, they may not have been able to break her out. Then again, I may have been put to a test I had no hope of passing when up against the vampires. At the moment, I could see no clear choice for what would have been the "right" answer. The best I could do now was deal with the aftermath and pray that we would finally succeed.

The four wolves suddenly turned and looked out the window, almost as a single unit. My gaze followed theirs, but I saw nothing. "What is it?" My voice came out as a whisper.

Rick, Isaiah, and David all stood up. "Shelby, stay here with Leah. We're going to go check it out."

Shelby and I immediately opened our mouths to protest, but stopped cold at the look on Isaiah's face. "Please, do as Rick says. We'll be careful, and Leah cannot afford to be alone right now. We'll be right back."

Torn between arguing and just doing what he asked to make this one thing easier for him, I bit down on the inside of my lip. From the corner of my eye, I saw Shelby nod, and I let my shoulders slump. He wasn't wrong when he said I didn't want to be alone, and I didn't think I had another battle in me just yet.

If anything, I wanted nothing more than to sleep for a week, then wake up to find out this had all been some sort of very extensive and realistic nightmare that my crazy brain had concocted after a night of staying up too late and eating too much cheese. The thought of cheese made my stomach sour.

"Do not, under any circumstances, let anyone in. For any reason." Rick sent Shelby to double check the front door. "With the Goddesses blessing you should be safe in the house. If something does happen, call for us and we will come right back, as fast as we can."

Shelby confirmed that the doors and windows were all shut and locked and that she had pulled the ground floor curtains in the main rooms. With that, the men slipped out the back door with the admonishment to lock it behind them. An eerie silence settled over the kitchen.

We watched them until they disappeared, which took all of three seconds. Then just blended into the trees as soon as they left the clearing. Together, we kept a sharp eye out for anything unusual.

"What do you think was out there?" The curiosity got the better of me and I had to ask. Without the sharp hearing, the wolves were blessed with I didn't have a clue. Had they not been here with me, I may not have even known anything was amiss until it was too late. It made me wish for a connection with my own wolf side.

"I'm not sure. It wasn't a distinctly identifiable sound. More like something that you could hear, but not quite place, and you could tell it just didn't belong."

She shrugged. The events of the day already had me on edge and I didn't even know the questions to ask to help myself understand.

"Have you ever dealt with vampires before?" The

word came out as a whisper, as if I feared they might hear me and I would draw their attention to us.

Shaking her head, she grimaced. "No, and I could have gone my whole life without ever encountering them and been happy about it. You've had more experience with them than me. What was it like?"

"I only saw him for a second. He was so fast. Unnaturally fast."

"Well, that makes sense. They are unnatural. They shouldn't even exist. After all, they're living dead things. What did it look like?"

"Surprisingly normal, for being dead? I mean, he had very pale skin and dark hair. I might not have thought anything about his appearance except that when he smiled, he actually had sharp teeth. Just like in the movies. Then he zipped down the hallway in a blur and took off out the front door. Poof, gone. If I'd seen him out and about on a normal day, I might have even found him attractive."

"So not the Count Dracula type ugly from the scary movies?"

"Nope, not the one I saw, anyways."

Boredom set in and we busied ourselves making cookies. I felt most comfortable in the kitchen where we had a better view of the forest and I attempted to calm my nerves by stress eating raw cookie dough. And a few cookies. We ate so much of the dough that we had to make a second batch to get enough cookies for the guys to have a few.

"Do you think they've been gone too long? Should we check on them?" The cookie dough could only subvert my natural anxiety for so long, and the worry began to settle in again.

"Nah, it really hasn't been that long. The sanctuary covers a lot of property, and they may have had to travel a little ways. Let's not worry until it starts getting closer to dark."

Her reasoning made sense, but the unease continued to grow. Knowing that not only did vampires exist, but that there could be one not far from us at that very moment gave me the willies. Add to that the fact that my very evil grandmother, who wanted nothing more than to kill me and suck my magic dry, once again roamed free and I was quickly becoming a basket case. Even with Shelby for company, I felt alone and exposed, despite being shut into a house protected by the very goddess that had created the sanctuary.

She sat at the table with a cup of coffee while I

washed dishes and wiped the counter repeatedly. She'd long since given up offering to help and I'd rebuffed her every suggestion for other activities to occupy my mind. Every little sound outside had me jumping out of my skin, and when I injured myself for the dozenth time Shelby took my arm and forced me to sit down.

"Leah. Talk to me. Tell me something about yourself that don't know. Talk to me about Aimee or your mom."

My breath wobbled as I exhaled, but her tactic was a good one. "Aimee and my mom didn't always see eye to eye. My mom's aversion to magic is the reason I was raised totally in the dark, and I had no idea that this world even existed. I didn't have any idea of this part of Aunt Aimee's life until she had already died. For the first little while, my mom still acted like I was crazy when I tried to talk to her about it."

Betrayal sliced through me as I thought about it. The memory of showing her what I'd learned in the attic and having her poo-poo it off, as if she hadn't a clue, still ate at me. All the while, she had known so much she could have shown me, even then. And she had chosen not to.

"Aimee lied to me about a lot of things, too. Like,

we all thought something terrible had happened to Rick, and he had disappeared from her life without a trace. I felt so badly for her, losing her husband when they were still newlyweds. And yet not only did he still live in the sanctuary, she knew it! And she saw him." I shook my head. "I know she had her reasons. But knowing she lied to me still stings. A lot."

"Wow. I bet. I'm so sorry." The look on Shelby's face made me wonder if she regretted opening this particular can of worms.

"It is what it is at this point. They're both dead. My grandmother, their very own mother, killed them." Saying it out loud in such a matter-of-fact manner drove the point home. My family was seriously messed up. Wow.

"I didn't know Aimee all that well, but everyone here knew how much she adored you. When you stopped coming to visit, she changed. There was a sadness that kind of hung about her."

"My not visiting started out as being my mom's fault, but I grew up. As an adult, I could have made it out here to visit her way more than I did. Something was always slightly more important, or had to be done right then, and I always promised we'd reschedule. Even the last email she sent me sat in my inbox, waiting for a reply because I was in a rush and I figured I could get to it later."

My eyes burned with the effort not to cry. I pictured her sitting at the computer and typing it out, then waiting for me to respond. The opportunity for me to tell her one last time that I loved her. To maybe make the plans that we might have kept this time. None of which would ever happen because I put it off and then she died.

My imagination showed me vivid pictures of her settling down at her desk after sending it and opening her email, looking for a reply from me. Maybe she even left the laptop on, so she'd hear a notification if an email came through. Then she'd be disappointed when it wasn't from me.

To make matters worse, her journal entry told me she had known. She was aware this fight with her very own mother could kill her, and still she respected my mother's wishes and didn't involve me, even though doing so might have saved her life. She sacrificed herself to keep me in the cocoon my mother had spun for me, away from magic.

Until Shelby moved closer and put her arms around

me, I didn't realize how hard I'd began to cry. The guilt ate at me like acid, slowly leeching the strength from me. The words poured out between hiccups and sniffles. I let every last ounce of guilt and shame out in a senseless torrent of words that probably didn't even make sense. Through it all, my friend sat by me, held me close and let me vent.

Once her shoulder was too wet to sop up any more tears, she substituted a kitchen towel and let me keep going. She didn't try and use words to comfort me or convince me I didn't have anything to feel guilty about. She just let me talk. The catharsis of letting it all go was magical in itself. And then it fed my anger.

The anger that this crazy ass woman, who we were related to, thought she could ruin the world of so many and just continue wreaking havoc with impunity. That she, who was really a nobody, had the nerve to think that all the people she wronged along the way were merely acceptable collateral damage who shouldn't have gotten in her way. Wiping away the tears and the snot, I looked Shelby in the eye.

"That bitch is done for. I've had it with her shit and I will be damned if she wins."

Before I could continue my tirade, I caught

movement out of the corner of my eye. The men were back, and I needed to know what they had found. Everything else could wait.

CHAPTER FOUR

The sight of them trudging across the clearing, dejected and somber, broke my heart before even hearing what they had to tell us. Their demeanor made the outcome of their search painfully obvious. Whatever they had found was not in our favor.

As they filed in and settled around the table, Shelby and I made cups of coffee to go with the plate of cookies we set out. Sometimes a little sugar rush made the bad things easier to deal with, in my opinion. Either way, I needed something to keep myself occupied while they gathered themselves in preparation for sharing whatever was out there.

With a deep breath, Rick looked over at Isaiah, who nodded, indicating he could begin. "We're not exactly sure what happened yet, but at least some of those who have gone missing are dead." Collecting himself, he continued. "We found multiple body parts, some of which we weren't even able to identify yet. It may take magic to do so."

"Oh no." Shelby and I whispered in tandem.

As bad as I thought it might be, hearing that something was killing people indiscriminately hadn't even been on my radar. The evil spirit hadn't been free for that long, so whatever had been murdering the pack members had begun to do so before she was sprung from her temporary prison.

Isaiah's grief and guilt bled through our bond, in spite of the fact that I could feel him desperately trying to keep it from me. These were his people, his friends. Without him saying a word, I knew he felt like he had failed them, and nothing I could say to him would relieve that guilt. Time and reaping justice were the only things that would temper their ferocity.

Unfortunately, I knew this from a similar experience.

"I'm sorry. I don't understand how you could not identify them. Isn't their scent enough? Or are they unfamiliar and not from your pack? Please forgive me if that is a rude question, but I don't quite understand how much of that works for you yet."

Isaiah took a deep breath as if to answer me, but Rick beat him to it. "Don't be sorry. The situation itself is quite strange. Normally, we would be able to identify them by scent. However, it almost seems as if their essence was tripped away from them. There is a void where there should be identifying markers. Some of them that we were able to identify were only because of tattoos, unique jewelry, or clothing articles that we recognized. I'm not even sure all of them are part of our pack, to be honest."

Tears slid down Shelby's cheeks, and I reached over to take her hand. "Who did you find? Who were you able to identify?"

Her voice shook as she forced the words out, and my heart broke for her. No doubt she knew all the victims from the sanctuary pack, and any one of them could have been close friend or even family. Even if it was someone she didn't particularly care for, her big heart would still be hurting for their loss.

David shifted his chair to be closer to her and put his arm around her shoulder, tugging at her until she leaned against him. Even though she resisted at first, I could tell it was because she was trying not to fall apart, not because she didn't want the comfort. The grief hanging on the air felt like being smothered with a hot, wet towel.

Even though the only members of the pack that I'd become truly close with sat at the table with me, I still dreaded hearing the names of those that had been lost. I'd met every single person who lived within the sanctuary at least once. We'd already lost so many during the skirmish before the packs united.

Thinking of that night reminded me of Ophelia's body in my attic, lying in stasis for the time I managed to learn to return her soul. We needed her now more than ever to help us out. I needed her knowledge and her guidance. Without her to teach me all the things I needed to know about the dark magic I'd acquired it would take me months, if not years, to master it. That would be months or years we didn't have to spare. The spell to reunite her soul with her earthly body needed to be my primary focus until I got it figured out.

"Earth to Leah?" Isaiah's voice penetrated my thoughts.

"Huh? I'm so sorry. I was just realizing that we really need Ophelia."

Rick and Isaiah both furrowed their brows at my announcement, and I inwardly grimaced at my loose lips. Both of them disagreed with my choice to try and reanimate Ophelia, which led to me trying not to mention it any more than necessary. I just needed to learn the ritual spells, gather the proper materials and get it done. Once successful, they wouldn't have anything to complain about and it would be over and done with.

All four of them stood and waited for me to pay attention. Rick and Isaiah exchanged glances, but didn't speak.

"Are you guys leaving?" Had I missed that much of the conversation?

Rick nodded. "Yes, we have some things to take care of back at the pack village. Will you be okay here, or do you want someone to stay with you?"

"I think the wards and protections are solid. I don't want to interfere with the things you need to, especially at a time like this. I will study the grimoires and see if I can find a way to help you identify the victims. Let me know if there is anything else I can do, okay?"

Shelby leaned in and wrapped her arms around me. "Will you be really be okay here alone? I can stay if you want."

Hugging her a little tighter, I shook my head. "You are absolutely welcome to stay if you need the distraction or just want my company, but I will be fine. I don't want to be the reason you miss out on being with your pack."

"I'll be back later, if that's okay?"

"Absolutely." I smiled at her. "You know you are welcome anytime."

As Shelby backed away, Isaiah took her place. He pulled me close and rested his cheek against the top of my head. "Will you really be okay? I hate leaving you here by yourself."

"Don't worry about me. We've already established that this is just about the safest place in the entire sanctuary. I won't go gallivanting about the woods or anything. I probably won't even go outside, and I promise not to open the door for anyone I don't know. Go be with your pack. Take care of your duties, and I'll be here waiting for you when you have time to return."

He kissed my cheek and stepped toward the door.

Rick fixed me with a stare. "Do exactly as you just said. Follow those plans and you should be perfectly safe. You can reach us in an instant if you need us, and we'll be here as fast as we can."

"Got it. I promise. You guys go take care of pack business while I do what I can from here."

David waved and led the foursome out the door. I threw the deadbolt behind them and sagged against the frame. Being alone in the house put my nerves on edge, but at the moment, I didn't feel any fear.

Yet.

Grabbing the stack of grimoires that Ophelia had lent me before her "death," I settled into the living room sofa with more cookies and more coffee. The caffeine would hopefully keep me from falling asleep and the sugar would feed my brain enough to hopefully find the information I needed. Instinct told me that without Ophelia's help, I wouldn't have the skills necessary to end the nightmare created by my grandmother's evil spirit, and we could not afford to fail.

Time drug on as I scoured the books for the ritual I needed. Despite the caffeination and consistent sugar intake, I must have dozed off, becoming aware of it only because I found myself in the misty dreamscape once more. Blowing out my breath, I found myself glad that I couldn't see my breath, which usually indicated something unpleasant was about to unfold.

"Hello?"

When no answer came, I frowned. Deciphering the purpose of the visit took time, and I didn't have much to spare. Those books needed to be read and I shouldn't have been falling asleep in the first place. If I learned anything from prior visits, though, I'd learned that things would happen in their own time and I had very little control while here.

"Hello? What do you want?" I tried being a little louder and a little more assertive in my question this time.

"Patience Leah. I am here."

I spun in a circle, seeing nobody. The voice echoed around me, making it impossible to tell which direction it came from. It sounded familiar, and I strained to see through the mist in hopes of placing a face to the sound.

"Do not look for me. I am here by projection only and cannot manifest a physical form here. I'd like to offer you more help."

"Goddess? Is that you?" I couldn't think of anyone else who might be inclined to help me, because the voice certainly didn't belong to my mother or Aunt Aimee.

"Yes, child, it is I. Time is running short. Your grandmother's spirit is gaining power even as we speak. Before long, she will be too powerful for even I to overtake her."

"How is that? You are a goddess and she's just a witch?"

"Yes, but I am imprisoned, and she has found ways to drain the power from others to strengthen herself. With the help of the vampires she has invited into the sanctuary, she is bleeding her victims dry of both their power and their blood."

"Imprisoned? I don't understand." My head spun. Since the beginning, I made the assumption that the goddess of the sanctuary resided here by choice, not force. Who on earth would be strong enough to imprison a goddess?

"We have little time, but I will tell you what I can. I've not always been the ruler here. This land was chosen, and the sanctuary created solely to act as my prison. At one time, I was free to go where and do as I pleased. I made a frightful enemy, and my soul is bound here to an oubliette beneath the ground on this peninsula."

Fear trickled down my spine. Did I feel sorry for her because she was stuck here, or afraid because she must have done something terrible to be given such a fate? She laughed softly, as if hearing the argument going on in my head.

Either way, I needed her help. Without it, my grandmother would win and I would die, along with most, if not all, of the residents of the sanctuary.

"Fear not, my darling. We are at an impasse. I need you just as much as you need me, and at this point, our only option is to work together. Without each other, we are both doomed to an unpleasant end. Our time here is almost over. I did not get to share everything I wished, but I will leave you with the information you seek. The ritual you seek is in the grimoire covered in the blackest black. You have the power to perform it. If you request my assistance I will do what I can, and I will come to you again..."

Her voice trailed off in my head as I felt myself crawling back toward wakefulness. Sitting upright with a jerk, I sent the stack of books next to me tumbling to the floor. Dropping to my hands and knees beside the couch, I rooted through the mess until I came up with the one she indicated held my answers.

The cover truly was of blackest black, seeming to absorb the light from the lamps around the room and swallow it whole. The leather under my fingers was smooth and supple, as if oiled regularly and not hundreds of years old. The only mar in its surface was a branded emblem I couldn't make out completely.

A shift back up to the couch brought sudden pain as my knee collided with the edge of the table. It tipped to the far side, sending everything on top of it sliding off, including my half-full coffee mug. Cussing, I limped to the kitchen for paper towels to sop up the mess, my knee throbbing the entire way there and back.

Coffee had splattered over a good number of the grimoires previously knocked to the floor and I spent more time than I would have liked ensuring I soaked up every last bit of the liquid from their covers and pages. Ophelia would be wanting these back when she returned, and she'd never let me borrow anything again if I returned them covered in beverage stains.

Once the majority of the mess had been toweled dry, I could finally turn my attention to the book that held my answers. If the goddess was correct. I'd been left confused over how an actual goddess could be imprisoned. Perhaps she wasn't as all-powerful as I had believed. After all, she claimed to need me just as much as I needed her, and something told me I didn't rate anywhere near goddess-level on the power scale.

For now, I would take her at her word. If the ritual I sought could be found in the black book, then I would find it. If not, my only option was to continue looking elsewhere. Not only did I need Ophelia's help, I owed it to her to bring her back. It was at least partly my fault she had died in the first place.

CHAPTER FIVE

For a brief moment, I feared what I would find when I opened the book. Would it be willing to reveal its secrets to me? Would it find me worthy of its knowledge? Or would this be one of those times where I would fall short, designated as one of the less-than and not enough?

Self-doubt wheedled its way into every thought. Goosebumps rose on my bare skin, the clammy sweat of my reluctance creating a sheen I could feel but not see. Closing my eyes, I attempted, rather pitifully, to talk myself down from the ledge on which I found myself poised. I'd come a long way in recent weeks. Endured relentless grief. Pitted myself against creatures I once believed to only exist in films and books.

And yet, when the time came to take a step as simple as opening a book, I faltered. The tapping of my foot against the floor created a muffled beat, mimicking the thudding of my heartbeat in my ears. My arms didn't seem to want to obey my brain. It took only a single motion to flip open the cover, and I struggled to do so.

With a burst of defiance, I pushed through the stranglehold my doubts had on my physical self and threw the cover open. Tilting my head downward, I promised myself I would open my eyes at the count of three. The title page or table of contents couldn't possibly be that scary. Perhaps at the count of five. But ten was a nice round number.

By the sheer resolve to save Ophelia, I managed to lift the eyelashes of my left eye, peeking ever so slowly at the book below. Both eyes popped open when it registered that there was nothing to be seen. The page contained no markings of any kind. Not words, or pictures, or even a smear of ink.

In disbelief, I rifled through the pages. Pristinely empty, every one.

"Damn it!" I let the book fall where it may in my lap and flopped backward, leaning my head against the couch.

Logic told me she wouldn't have lent me an empty book. However, I needed to decipher how to access the secrets hidden inside. But how?

After attempting a couple of easy spells to reveal the contents, I paused. It would be just my luck the thing was like a cell phone and if you input the wrong thing too many times, you'd be locked out, probably forever. Desperation gnawed at my gut like a beaver sawing logs. Now what?

Ophelia no doubt figured she would be around to help me when I got to this particular stage of my research and study, which explained why she never told me its secret access code. Or even mentioned that it needed one. If it was keyed to members of her coven or family, I might never get it open. Unless...

Grabbing the book, I headed for the stairs. After slamming my very-not-funny bone on the railing when turning on the light and stubbing my right big toe twice, I reached the attic. The sight of her still form just laying there, seemingly in a deep sleep, slammed into me. The spell had healed her physical wounds to sight, but I knew how precarious her situation was.

The spell would not preserve her forever. And if I could not find the way to bring her back, her soul could be trapped forever. My rash decision had the potential to sentence her to a fate worse than death.

No pressure, right?

Book clutched to my chest, I eased down onto the floor beside her. Reaching out, I ran my fingers over her sleeve.

"I need your help." While just a whisper, the words seemed to echo through the attic, bouncing off the beams. "Please. I don't know what to do and the goddess said this is the book I need. I can't figure out how to access it."

Silence greeted my pleas, not that I expected anything else. A dead body couldn't speak. Laying my hand on her arm, I tried touching the pages of the book at the same time. Nothing. Moving my hand so skin met skin, I tried again. Nada.

Frustration ate at me. Leaning forward, I lay my head against her, sobbing. The only words I could find were those of apology. The lengthy list of things I wanted to apologize for seemed unending. When I couldn't think of any new things, I resorted to repeating myself. Time slipped by. I knew that I didn't have the time to spare, but I lacked the emotional bandwidth to drag myself out of the funk I'd allowed my brain to fall into.

When the tears finally ran dry and my inner eyelids resembled twenty grit sandpaper, I finally lifted my head. During my sob-fest, I must have knocked the book over, as it lay open, leaning against her leg. The page presenting itself was covered in writing. Tiny letters left minimal margins and filled it from top to bottom.

Snatching it off the floor, I breathed a sigh, so thankful that something somewhere heard my prayers. Until the words faded from existence right before my eyes. One second they were visible, and the next they ceased to exist.

"No! Please come back! Please."

Staring at the once-again blank page, I let my temper take the reins and chucked the book as hard as I could. It bounced off a stack of boxes and lay open on the floor. The bare parchment mocked me.

Scrubbing my hands against my face, I tried to rub away the failure. Exhaustion ate at me. Naps alone were not enough to sustain me, especially as my slumber got constantly interrupted by other-worldly players who seemed to think that whatever they had to say to me negated my need for restful sleep.

Perhaps somewhere a spell existed that could make sleep unnecessary. But until I ran across it, I somehow needed to find a way to get uninterrupted time to recharge my body. Pushing myself off the floor, I groaned as my body protested the request to bear my weight. Before I could walk over to pick up the grimoire and get back at it, my legs gave out.

With nothing to support me, I tumbled to the floor, sprawling across Ophelia's still form. Mortified, I rolled sideways, apologizing again despite knowing not only could she not hear me, she didn't feel the crush of our collision. The bruises blooming on my skin would not be matched by any mark marring hers. She, at least, was protected by the spell.

Grimacing, I scooted over to the book and scowled at it. Gathering it up, I slammed the cover closed and bit my lip until it bled. My eyes rolled so far back into my head that it hurt. Why would it tease me with a glimpse of the writing and then vanish?

A tiny squeak distracted me from my woes and I

looked around the room for the creator of the sound. On a beam at the far end of the attic, the single remaining chipmunk peered cautiously from a hole in the wall. Poor thing, I'd probably terrified it half to death with my tantrum.

"I'm sorry, little one. I didn't mean to disturb you. It's alright, you can come out if you want. I'm just frustrated. I'm certainly not angry at you."

With slow steps, he (or she) ventured further out on to the beam, eyeing me with distrust. In an effort not to create any more fear, I sat absolutely still and waited until they felt comfortable. Within minutes, my furry little friend sat on the wooden plank floor only a foot or two from me.

"I can't figure out how to make this stupid book show me the contents. For just a second they were there and then when I picked it up, every single marking disappeared. Poof. Gone."

Giggling at myself for talking out my woes with the chipmunk, I stopped, and we stared at each other for a few seconds. It crept closer, sniffing at the book. Then it turned and inhaled deeply at Ophelia's leg. Back and forth, it ran between Ophelia and the grimoire. Snuffling and chortling. The behavior continued as I grew increasingly curious about its actions. Finally, the little critter grew impatient and stopped between the two, chattering loudly.

I frowned. "What?"

For the first time in my life, I believed I had made a rodent disappointed in me. I'd disappointed many people. Probably a few dogs and cats even, but never a chipmunk. Raising my eyebrows in question didn't seem to have any effect.

"I'm sorry. I don't understand."

These one-sided conversations made me feel a little crazy. Who in their right mind communed with creatures that couldn't talk back? Besides myself, of course.

The animal heaved what could only be described as a sigh and stalked over to the book, chattering loudly. It then quieted down, stalked over to Ophelia's still form, and chattered again. Back and forth, back and forth. Ridiculously long moments passed before the light bulb finally came on.

"Of course! Thank you."

Shifting back to sit next to the pile of blankets, I propped the book against Ophelia, leaning it open against her side. Sure enough, within seconds, the writing once more appeared. She probably had some way of keeping the contents visible as she worked with it, but for now, I needed to keep it in contact with her in order to read it.

"I owe you a great big snack."

With a sniff my tiny friend turned its back on me and clambered up to the beam it emerged from previously, tail puffed. One final squeak and he or she disappeared from my sight.

Relief flooded me. Time ceased to exist as I scanned each individual page, looking for the answers I needed to bring Ophelia back to me. No table of contents was included, so each entry had to be read before I could know if it held the spell I searched for.

Everything else got shut out as I read. At some point, I felt Isaiah venture close to the house, but he didn't come in, so I shoved his presence away and continued to focus solely on my priority. He'd come find me if he needed to.

Three quarters of the way through the book, I began to get despondent. A number of hours had passed as I searched, and I was running out of book. If I couldn't identify the ritual spell in the one I would have no other choice but to spend even more time digging through the others. Time I knew I didn't have.

About ten pages from the back cover, the writing ran out. The pages just became blank. Had someone stopped entering spells before they ran out of room, or did it require something more to become available to me? Perhaps physical contact wasn't enough, for the most important of information would be revealed.

Tears fell. Now what? All this time wasted, and I got nothing in return. The only other person I could turn to for advice was Rick. He knew her before I came along and maybe, just maybe, he could give me more insight into how her magic worked. If he couldn't, we were all screwed.

Reaching out through our mental communication, I inquired whether he could swing by the house and help me with something. As usual, he agreed to assist in whatever way he could. I gathered the book and prepared to meet him in the kitchen. It took most of my strength to unfold my aching limbs and lumber to the stairway.

Supporting the majority of my weight with the arm and hand using the handrail, I still needed to use the arm holding the book to steady myself against the wall. If my knees or hips gave out on me now, I had no way to stop myself from tumbling to the bottom. At I would have to hope for nothing breaking and accept the aches and pains that would follow me for the forseeable future.

Rick made it in through the back door from wherever he'd been before I managed to get to the table. He raised his eyebrows at my state and I shrugged.

"It's been a long day. Very, very long."

"I can see that. What have you been up o since we left, and what can I help you with?"

Taking a deep breath, I launched into my dilemma.

CHAPTER SIX

Rick's eyes squinted as he lowered his brows. For a moment, he did nothing more than stare at me silently. Exhaling loudly, he plopped into the kitchen chair and gestured for me to do the same. Wanting his help, I obliged, although I wanted nothing more than to take him back up to the attic and have him help me pull the knowledge from the book.

"Leah..."

Putting my hand up, I cut him off before he could get started. "Look. I know you disagree with my choice.

You've made yourself very clear. Putting the fact that we need her help aside, think about this. At this point, if I do not reunite her soul with her body, I am leaving it to float in limbo. That is beyond unfair to her."

Using both hands, he rubbed his face, and I could practically feel him arguing with himself. He knew that I wasn't wrong. And he'd liked Ophelia enough to not want to cause her any torment, especially after all the help she already gave. She'd willingly given her life to fight on our side in a war that wasn't hers to fight.

"As you know, I am not familiar with much of her dark spirit magic. The one thing I can tell you, if you haven't tried it already, is that much of it is rooted in blood magic. These particular pages may need her blood to unlock them."

A shudder wracked my body. "I have to cut her?"

He paired an apologetic look with a shrug. "I'm sorry. I told you I didn't know much about it. But she often pricked her finger or sliced her palm if she was doing a spell. If that doesn't work, it will take more research than just asking me to get any answers."

The thought turned over in my mind. "Her physical body is in stasis. Will it even bleed?"

"I'm sorry. Once again, I don't know. All you can do

is try."

"Will you come up to the attic with me while I do it?"

He stood up from the kitchen chair, and I briefly thought he would head toward the attic stairs. Instead, he reached for the knob of the back door.

"Again, I'm sorry. But I'm not comfortable with that. I really don't want to be a party to this, and if I could free her soul without dragging it back into her body, I would."

An uncontrollable flinch jerked my head back. For a moment I don't think I would have been any more surprised if he had slapped me across the face. It seems that his aversion to what I had done to our friend didn't really register until right that moment.

"Don't be sorry. I do understand. I appreciate that you have been willing to help me as much as you have."

He smiled at me sadly. "In this case, my goal is to help her, and it seems the only way to do that is to help you right now. Call me if you need help – with anything else – and I'll come back. But for right now, I have some things I need to do."

"Okay, thanks again for doing this, even though you didn't want to."

The back door latched closed behind him and I watched him walk across the clearing and onto the path leading into the woods. It pained me that I caused him distress for asking him to help me, but, truth be told, I didn't have anyone else who could answer the question for me.

Standing there at the back door, I took a minute to close my eyes and offer up a plea for forgiveness. Perhaps what I had done was wrong, but it was done now and I needed to right the situation, whatever it cost me. Her soul would not be condemned to limbo. Not if I had any say in the matter. If adding her blood to the mix did not reveal that which I needed to know, I would have to return to our secret room in the basement and attempt to contact the goddess for more assistance.

Grabbing a bottle of pain reliever and a soda, I downed a handful. Leaving the soda on the table, I once more picked up the book, wincing at the pain in my elbow and shoulder and drug myself back down the hall to the attic stairs. The flight looked interminably long and by the time I made it to the top; I huffed and puffed as if I had just run a marathon. Every part of my body hurt in a multitude of ways.

Settling myself on the floor once more, I leaned the

book against her and flipped to the first blank page. Steeling myself to gather the nerve to slice open my totally defenseless friend, I realized I had forgotten to grab something sharp to do the deed. My groan bounced off the attic walls. It seemed rather unlikely that I could get to the kitchen and back again, but I had no other option. Even if I found something that would work up here, I'd never cut her, even the tiniest of slices, without making sure it was clean.

Gathering what little will power remained, I scooted closer to the piles of trunks near the wall and used their stability to stand myself up. My legs needed a minute to get the jiggly gelatin feeling under control, and once I felt reasonably sure I wouldn't collapse, I headed for the steep stairs.

Unfortunately, my confidence exceeded my ability and, on the attempt to traverse the very first step, my right leg decided it had enough and crumpled under me. Multiple parts of my tumbling body felt every single riser on the way down, and whatever hadn't been in pain before the fall was now throbbing in agony.

My eyelids dropped closed of their own accord, and I didn't even try to move until the rushing in my ears quieted some. My joints were on fire, my head ached, and I could feel blood dripping near my temple. While the pain induced perspiration as well, I could tell it was blood from the thick texture and coppery smell.

When I swallowed, I almost choked, because apparently something inside my mouth bled too. It hurt to gag, and I just gave up. Until some of the pain abated, I planned to just lay on the floor and rest. This time there would be no getting up, no matter how badly I wanted to try and decipher the grimoire.

Unable to even shift my body enough to straighten out, I lay on the hall floor, drifting in and out of sleep. Or maybe consciousness. Who knows? The pain seemed to be increasing instead of improving, but my stubborn streak meant avoiding a call for help unless no other choice made itself available.

The back door opened and closed after some time, and my brain was still so foggy I couldn't even register who entered until I heard Isaiah call my name.

The first go at answering him squeaked out as nothing more than a whisper, and by the time I gathered enough energy to try again, I could see him coming down the hall in my direction. His legs, anyways. It hurt too much to turn my head and look up at him.

"Leah! Oh my goodness, are you alright? What

happened?"

"Stairs," I whispered. "Fell."

"Is anything broken? Do you want me to help you get up?"

Without thinking, I tried to shake my head and just cried when the motion shot pain through me. "No, please. Hurts too much."

"I need to get you off this floor. I'm going to pick you up, as gently as I can, and take you to your bed."

I wanted to argue. I really did, but I didn't have it in me. At that point I didn't even know how long I'd been laying there and despite knowing it would hurt like the dickens, I really did want to get off the hard surface.

When he picked me up, I whimpered, but bit my tongue to avoid complaining. Thanks to his long legs, we were only a few strides from my bedroom door, but they felt like the longest few seconds I had in a while. Concentrating on being grateful he showed up when he did, I managed to not cry out when he laid me down, even though I wanted to.

He disappeared through the doorway and returned some time later with a washcloth and a bowl of warm water, plus an ice pack, a drink and the bottle of pain relief I left on the table earlier. Once the dried blood washed away, he inspected the injury and smiled at me gently.

"It's not as bad as it looked at first. Although I think everything looks a little worse when you are sprawled out on the floor and not really conscious."

Knowing I couldn't force my face into a smile, I just sighed. "I suppose, but unconscious is better than dead, and I am pretty sure I didn't break anything. I just feel like I've been run over by a Mack truck, is all. Going eighty miles an hour. With snow studs on the tires. And then maybe struck by lightning."

"Ah, there's the drama I've come to expect from you. Now I know you're going to be just fine after some rest."

"I can't. I don't have time to rest."

"Leah, you probably can't even get out of this bed yourself, much less back up the stairs. Or were you headed down for something?"

Too exhausted to come up with a fib on the spot, I settled for telling him where I'd been going, but not why. Unfortunately, he knows better than to take my vague answer at face value and insisted I tell him the entire story.

By the time I got to the end, I couldn't even hold my

eyes open anymore. I missed the majority of what he said after, only jerking back to attention when I heard him huff in indignation.

"Fine, I can tell you are falling asleep, and I am going to let you because you need it, but we are going to finish this conversation when you wake up, and don't you think for a second I'll forget. I'll be in the living room in case you need something."

With his parting shot, he left the room, pulling the door closed but not latching it, presumably so he could hear me if I tried to call out. Seconds later, all thought vanished, and I fell into a deep sleep.

Drifting in and out of the dreamscape told me someone wanted to make contact, but my injuries and prior exhaustion left me so disoriented that I couldn't maintain a connection. It didn't matter if the dreamscape held the goddess, my evil grandmother, or even my mom. I had nothing left in the tank to give and whatever it was would have to wait until I did.

At some point, even the dreamscape disappeared, and I sank blissfully into total blackness. No pain, no thoughts, and no interruptions. A brief peek at the window upon my next waking told me the sun just peaked over the horizon and I didn't need to get up yet if I didn't want to. And boy, did I not want to. If such a thing was even possible, my body hurt more after resting than it had right after my fall.

It took nothing more than letting my eyelids fall closed once more for me to sleep again. This time, however, I did dream. Or more accurately, I had a nightmare. I dreamt of sitting next to Ophelia and trying to open the book. As soon as I pricked her finger, I knew I'd been right and blood did not leak from the tiny wound.

Frowning, and whispering an apology, I squeezed gently, just enough to get a single drop of blood. Praying I wouldn't need a new drop for every page I wanted to look at, I smeared the crimson droplet onto the first page.

The words appeared, just as I hoped. Then the book burst into flames.

CHAPTER SEVEN

Isaiah loomed above me, calling my name when I opened my eyes. It took a second for my vision to focus and my eyelids fluttered rapidly as they tried to wipe the fuzzies from my sight. His face swam into focus and I sat up with a start, terrified that the dream may have been some sort of premonition.

Squeaking in pain, I pushed at him, feebly attempting to get him out of the way so I could check the attic. If the book caught fire while leaning against Ophelia's body, we would lose her forever and her soul would be lost. The stasis spell held her body in its original state, but I didn't know if it would protect her from harm.

"I need to get up to the attic! I have to check on the book and Ophelia!"

"Slow down." He pushed me back against the pillows. "What are you worried about? I can't think of a single good reason you should be getting out of bed just yet."

"The dream. I have to make sure it was just a dream."

"What dream? Slow down."

With my weakened state, he didn't even struggle to keep me against the mattress, despite the effort I put into getting up. Within a minute, my strength abandoned me and I quit trying to get out of bed. Instead, I begged him to go up to the attic for me and look. He resisted.

"There is no way anything caught fire. We'd smell the smoke and the fire alarms would be going off. I promise you, nothing is on fire up there."

"Please? For me? I won't be able to relax until I know for sure. You could bring the book back downstairs to me and then I would have nothing to worry about."

"Leah, no. You know how I feel about seeing her lying there, and I am absolutely *not* touching that book. It gives me the creeps."

A tear slid down my cheek. My head knew he wasn't wrong, but the fear that lingered after the dream smothered me. I'd never forgive myself if I ruined our only chance of helping Ophelia.

"That's not fair! No emotional warfare."

"I'm sorry," I sniffed. "I'm not trying to cry. Just ignore it. I couldn't help it. The dream seemed so real. I'll be fine in just a minute."

"Are you hungry? Thirsty? What can I get you?"

"Honestly? I think I just need more ibuprofen and something to wash it down with."

"You got it. Anything else?"

"Maybe an ice pack for my head? Everything hurts. I hate to be whiny, but my entire body is just throbbing from head to toe."

"Don't worry about it. I'll grab one. Be right back."

Without his presence to keep me occupied, I slid right back into a light sleep. The next time I woke, Isaiah sat in the chair beside my bed, eyes closed. The ice pack, now warm, rested on my forehead and the ibuprofen and glass of water sat on the nightstand.

Rolling to my side caused muscle cramps and sent me into a spin with even my eyelids twitching. Once they subsided, I continued my journey to reach the bedside table and get some pain relief on board without waking Isaiah.

That plan flew out the window as soon as my hand reached the glass. Another spasm racked my body, and I backhanded the water, sending it flying, cup and all, right into Isaiah's lap and soaking his crotch. He startled awake with a yelp, jumping out of the chair faster than I'd ever seen him move. If I hadn't been in so much pain, I would have laughed until I peed my own pants.

By the time I managed to focus on him, I did indeed laugh, despite the pain. The incredulous look on his face left me with no other option.

"What was that for?"

Struggling to get the words out between giggles and winces, I just kept it simple. "Accident. Sorry. Muscle spams."

He shook his head and rolled his eyes. He reached out and helped me get into a sitting position before handing me the ibuprofen. "I'll get you some more water, just a minute."

Upon his return, I got the medicine down and then sent him on his way. "Go get dry pants. Or I can find you some sweats that will probably fit and we can throw your jeans in the dryer."

"I should probably go back and check on things. Will you be okay by yourself?"

"Sure. For now, my only goal is to get a shower. The hot water will probably help the muscle pain, and I can always sit down if I start feeling weak or shaky."

He left, and I crawled out of the bed and hobbled down the hall to the shower. By the time the water ran cold, I could honestly say I felt better than when I got in. Dressing in a comfortable sweatsuit I headed, very slowly, back to the attic. I needed to know if her blood would be the key, and if I could get any blood out of her at all.

Despite my fears after the nightmare, the book sat just as I left it, leaned up against her thigh with zero sign of smoke or flames. Turning the pages, I verified the words still existed, and they did, thank the goddess. Taking the small paring knife I remembered to grab from the kitchen, I took her hand closest to me and held it gently.

"I'm sorry. You have to know that I hate to do this,

but I haven't found any other choice at the moment. I'm sorry I did this to you to begin with, but at this point, I will do whatever it takes to make sure your soul does not wander aimlessly for eternity. You're welcome to slap the shit out of me once we get you awake, okay?"

Rubbing the pad of my thumb along hers, I hesitated, unable to bring myself to make even the tiniest mar on her flesh. I'd never purposely cut anyone open in my life. Unfortunately, I knew no other way to get any blood for the book.

Apologizing one last time, I used the very tip of the knife to place a tiny prick at the tip of her thumb. My worst fears became realized when no blood welled to the surface. I couldn't even see a red mark where I had poked her. Again, I found myself crying quietly.

In the middle of my pity party, I heard whispers in my ear. "Don't give up. You can do it."

Setting Ophelia's hand gently back on her stomach, I turned in a complete circle and confirmed that I was, indeed, alone in the attic. After spending some time questioning my sanity, I once more grabbed her hand and held it tightly. The voice was right. I could do it. I just couldn't give up.

Taking the knife, I used the tip to make a slightly

deeper puncture. When the wound remained dry, I apologized to her once more and gave the skin a squeeze. My reward? A brilliant scarlet droplet. Just once, and not a very big one, but I had blood. Praying it would unlock the words, I pressed it to the page.

Nothing happened at first, but words slowly shimmered to the surface, as if rising from deep dark water. Testing the strength of the blood droplet, I flipped through the next few pages and squealed to see words on each page.

Upon skimming each page, nothing jumped out as being "the one," so I went back to the first page and read through word for word. On the very last page, second to last paragraph, I found the information I'd been searching for. Thrilled to have an answer, I deflated slightly when I realized that instead of the actual answer, the entry revealed only the location to the true answer.

I somehow needed to get Ophelia's body back to the cave that held the altar.

Unsure of how long the blood would keep the words visible, I hunted down some paper and a pen and transcribed everything related to finding the spell that I might need. I wanted a portable version that wouldn't require me to poke her thumb any more. I'd managed out of desperation the first time, but I never wanted to have to do that to anyone, ever again.

Contemplating the passage I'd just read, it occurred to me how odd it seemed that I needed to take her to an altar tied to the crescent magic and that of the sanctuary when the ritual was rooted decidedly in the dark spirit magic. Not being in a position to argue, I just told myself to follow the instructions and not ask questions.

Kissing her gently on the forehead, I took the book, my paper and headed back down to the kitchen. My stomach had been rumbling for the last little while, but I ignored it in the search for answers. At this point, if I didn't eat something, I might pass out.

Knowing that neither one would be excited to help me, I still reached out to Rick and Isaiah. Without help, I couldn't get Ophelia to the cave by myself. I just didn't have the strength. Both of them agreed to come and have breakfast with me, so as I waited, I began preparing food.

The table held plates of bacon, hash browns, toast and fried eggs when they came walking across the clearing together. Everyone got served food and coffee before I launched into my plea for help.

"So. I need your help."

The two of them exchanged glances, but neither of them said a word and just shoveled food into their mouths as they waited for me to explain further.

"Rick, your suggestion was the right one. It worked, and I found the answers I needed."

"That's great, but what could you need help with? Neither of us can wield magic, so we can't possibly help you with the ritual."

"Well, you're partially right, and partially wrong. The ritual instructions can only be found in the cave that once held the altar. I can't even get the entire spell until I get her there. I don't yet understand if I will need to complete the ceremony in the cave or not."

Isaiah wrinkled his face and redirected his attention to the plate in front of him. Rick sighed. He might not be pleased, but he had already agreed to help me, since he couldn't help Ophelia any other way.

Rick looked at Isaiah and shrugged his shoulders. "You don't need to join us on this mission. I know how you feel about the entire situation, and I'd never ask you to move a body."

"No, no. I need to come. I think I need to be close to

Leah right now, whether I like the mission or not."

"Wow, thanks for making it seem like such a chore."

The two of them bickered back and forth, and I decided to just let them argue while I ate my own food. As long as someone would help me to get her where I needed her to be, I wasn't going to complain. Beggars can't be choosers and all that jazz.

Eventually, the arguing turned to the logistics of getting her there. I interjected occasionally, but they didn't seem to want my opinions. Rick decided to send someone trustworthy ahead to the cave and have them clean it up and prepare for our arrival. We agreed since the trip would be slow going, we would leave first thing the next morning.

That meant our arrival would fall sometime in the early afternoon, which would hopefully leave me enough time to prepare for the ritual. From most of the experience I'd had with Ophelia's type of magic, I figured the magic would work best near the middle of the night. If we got lucky, I'd be able to find the instructions and perform the magic tomorrow night, and not have to waste any time waiting for the next one.

We decided to spend the rest of the day preparing

for the trip. Without being able to see the entire spell until we reached the cave, I wanted to pack anything and everything that I could possibly need. Well, almost. I didn't want the reason we couldn't finish the ritual to be that I didn't have one of the spell ingredients or focus objects. Even if we wound up not needing many of the things that I packed, I'd definitely rather have them and not need them than need them and not have them.

Once I gathered the majority of the items I suspected I would need, I took a break and went out to sit between my mother and my aunt's graves. If anyone could guide me from beyond, it would be one of the two of them.

CHAPTER EIGHT

The sun was on its way down when Rick came walking around the side of the building. He paused briefly when he saw me sitting at the gravesides. After a short hesitation, he headed over.

"Am I interrupting something?"

"Nah, come on over. I'm just trying to get some of my thoughts in order, and it seemed the logical question would be, what would Aimee do? And then I figured that my mom might have some sort of influence, so why not?"

He barked out a laugh. "What would Aimee do? She'd be absolutely thrilled to know that is what you use as a compass for determining the best course of action on something."

"She would, wouldn't she?" My eyes welled up unexpectedly. "I miss her so damn much."

He pursed his lips before answering. "I know. I do too."

We sat in silence together, both of us lost in our own thoughts. Taking a deep breath, I swallowed my grief and tried to move on.

"Is there anything else I can do to help everything be ready for tomorrow?"

He shook his head. "I came looking for you to tell you that everything is under control and all we have to do tomorrow is wake up and start walking."

"How will we get her there?"

"Some of the guys offered to take turns carrying her, but we decided that a stretcher would make it easier for everyone. We can take turns carrying her, and the burden divided between the two will be much easier. While any one of us could carry her, we'll move quicker with less strain on each person."

"That does make sense. The rest of us will carry the

backpacks with supplies."

"That's exactly what we were figuring." He turned as if to leave.

"Hey, Rick?"

He spun back around to look at me. "What's up?"

"Can I ask you something?"

"Of course you can. What's up?"

"Do you think I should tell Isaiah to stay here? I feel like maybe the pack will need him to be here, and we both know he really doesn't want to be a part of this to begin with. I know he was angry over my decision, even though he didn't come right out and say it."

"I think we need to allow him to make his own decisions. I'm not his boss, and neither are you."

My exhale drug on until I worried I wouldn't be able to pull any air back in. Sucking in a deep breath, I bit my lip and chewed it for a second before replying. "I know. I just feel like I am forcing the issue a little bit. I get that everybody thinks I was in the wrong. Even I am not convinced I'm not. But it's done, and there is no way I am going to let her soul be in purgatory forever."

"I understand how you feel. Sometimes, during an overwhelming or particularly painful situation, we do things we might not consider otherwise. I think you are doing the right thing by moving forward and ensuring her spirit will be reunited for her body. Isaiah is just having a more difficult time confronting his feelings. There may be a reason in his past that is coloring his view of the situation."

"I didn't even think of that. And you are right. I am far from being in charge of anyone else's choices. Hell, I've proven that there is a good argument. I shouldn't even be in charge of my own!"

He reached down and squeezed my shoulder. "You're doing a fine job, and don't you let that little voice in your head tell you any different."

"Thank you. I just really wish that I wasn't having to learn to make them in life or death situations. Especially when it involves the life or death of others."

"I know, kiddo. I do. But you're doing great and every single one of us is genuinely doing the very best we can with the hand we've been dealt. Things are going to work out."

"I think my best course of action for this evening is to eat a good meal and rest. I'm still awfully sore."

He reached down to help pull me to my feet. "Isaiah told me you fell down the stairs?"

"I should learn by this point that running myself

ragged helps nobody, and actually does more harm than good. I lost a lot of hours just trying to recuperate, and that's with my increased healing abilities. I need to be ready for tomorrow."

"I'd offer to wait another day, but I know how you feel about losing any more time."

"Thanks, but I'll be fine. If I get too tired, I'll just crawl up with Ophelia and take a nap."

He laughed good and hard at that one. "You're welcome to see if they're willing to carry you, but it will probably cost you."

We went our separate ways as he headed into the woods and I climbed the steps to the back door. Sitting expectantly on the small table was my single chipmunk friend. The sight of him brought a smile to my face.

"I owe you a snack, don't I? I'll be right back."

Slipping through the back door, I collected a small bowl and filled it with crackers, grapes, and a few cookies. Frowning at the excess sugar, I popped a couple of the cookies in my own mouth and traded them for a hunk of bagel.

"Here you go, little fella. Thank you so much. We're taking off tomorrow, but I'll be back in a day or two. Be safe."

The silence in the house seemed strange to me, but not in a bad way. After a brief dinner, I decided to grab a pillow and blanket and go down to the basement to try and sleep in our hidden room. While not as comfortable as I bed, I figured it gave me the best chance of getting restful sleep. My hope was that the only figure able to get into my dreams in there would be the goddess herself, and I welcomed any opportunity to gather more information from her.

Checking that every door and window remained locked and secured, I made sure Isaiah knew that I'd be sleeping in the connection room so would be out of contact for the rest of the night. Feeling restless and not quite ready to sleep, I also gathered some snacks, a soda and a book. While wanted to bring the grimoires and see what else I could learn, I felt like it would be disrespectful to the goddess, and therefore picked some light reading material instead.

The night passed peacefully, with no dreamy interruptions, even from the goddess herself. By the time the others arrive to get Ophelia ready to travel, I'd been up for a while and had my coffee. Passing out mugs to the others before we left, I surveyed the hustle and bustle. So much lay on the line for today's journey.

Isaiah didn't show until we had everything gathered in the clearing and were ready to head out. I left a last treat for my rodent friend and double checked to be sure the house got locked up. I felt a little ridiculous doing it, but it gave me some peace to feel I'd done what I could to protect the house. All of Ophelia's very heavy grimoires lay at the bottom of my backpack. Nothing could have convinced me to leave them behind.

Before heading onto the trail, we stood in the clearing, deciding who would spend the first rotation as their animal, which Rick and Isaiah both agreed would be safer with all that happened recently. Barely twenty feet up the trail, a dark wolf came running up on the group, startling me. In wolf form, I could only recognize a few people.

As I jumped back, Isaiah put his hand up. "It's okay, it's David."

Wolf-David stopped in front of Isaiah, and I waited patiently for them to have their conversation. The look on Isaiah's face told me the news wasn't good. He turned to me with a look on his face that screamed devastation.

"What? What is it?"

Before uttering a word, he reached out and took my hand. "Shelby has gone missing. I'm sorry."

Snatching my hand back, I yelled at him before I thought about the words that came out of my mouth. "What are you doing still standing here? You need to find her!"

"I'm not leaving you. If I go find her, then you need to stay here."

"No. I don't have time for that. Ophelia doesn't have time either. I have to get this done. I can't wait any longer."

"Then I go with you and the others can look for her. I'm not compromising on this."

His stubbornness took my breath away. My eyes locked with his and I took a deep breath.

"If you don't go look for her, and I find out that you could have saved her, I will never speak to you again. Ever."

His eyes went wide at my tone and he opened his mouth to argue, but I turned my back on him. As I walked down the trail, I threw my last comment to him back over my shoulder.

"This time I'm the one not compromising. As a matter of fact, you are not welcome to join us. Now go."

The others took time to catch up with me, except for Rick, and I assumed they checked with him for permission before continuing. Tears streamed down my cheeks. One of the few friends I had. If I lost her too, I didn't know if I could take it.

We needed to get Ophelia to the altar and bring her back to us. Maybe she would be able to help us find Shelby, and anyone else still missing. For a long portion of the hike, I walked ahead of the others, praying to the goddess to bring Shelby back to us. Rick gave me some space and then came up to talk to me.

"We're going to stop for a minute so we can change everyone's positions. It's going to be okay. We will find her."

"But what if we don't? All those others have gone missing and many of them are dead."

"Have faith. Sometimes when we are in the middle of something difficult, that is all that we can do. We have to believe that we can influence the outcome and our prayers will be answered."

"That seems a little bit like setting myself up for a painful failure if I'm wrong."

"In this life, there are no guarantees. We will go through things that will make us hurt. You've unfortunately had a trial by fire in that lesson over the last few weeks. But holding onto hope is what keeps the unknown from crippling us. What you're about to do is very important. Shelby would never want to know that you didn't give it one hundred percent of your attention because of her. Don't force her to feel guilty about anything if -when- she returns to us."

Damn it. Of course, he made sense. Getting the obvious spelled out for you always sucked. "I probably owe Isaiah an apology."

Rick smiled. "It wouldn't hurt for you each to offer one. He wasn't in the right in this situation, either. Worry and stress can change people for brief times, not necessarily for the better. As long as both people are forgiving, it usually works out okay."

"Thank you."

As the team shifted positions and traded jobs, we stood in companionable silence. Mulling over what he told me, I contemplated reaching out to Isaiah, but decided to wait until we arrived at the East village. It gave him a chance to calm down and also time to gather more information, so hopefully he would have some news to share as well.

From the group behind us, one of the wolves let out a sudden yelp. Rick spun around faster that I'd ever seen him move and raced back towards the one who made the sound. The others turned in circles, looking for the source of the trouble, but I couldn't see anything.

The entire group circled up, protecting the people carrying the stretcher and whining for me to join them. Using my magic, I reached out to the forest around us, looking for the enemy. At first, I found nothing at all. Eventually, that clued me in to begin looking for the anomalies that were *not* present.

Strange blank spots in the surrounding trees gave the stalkers away. Pouring more magic into my request, I demanded to know who we were dealing with. The coppery tang of blood bloomed in my mouth.

Shit. Vampires. And more than one.

CHAPTER NINE

"Vampires!" I shouted the word out loud to make sure everyone in the party knew what we were dealing with, and to let the attackers know that I knew.

They tried incredibly hard to conceal themselves, and it pleased me to let them know that their skills were far from enough when it came to dealing with me. Unfortunately, the others had no way to sense where the bloodthirsty creatures were hiding, for they had somehow managed to block every scent from even the wolves' noses.

The group of us stood still in the circle, waiting for them to make a move, with nobody but me able to tell when one decided to come closer. For some time, the two groups were at a standstill. We did not try to proceed, and they didn't come any closer.

Finally, after what felt like forever, a single creature crept up from behind. My vocal warning proved not to be enough, and poor Evan, at the very back of the pack, still wound up with bloody gashes down his arm. Thankfully, he managed to avoid them catching him at the throat.

In my attempt to watch for each attacker and warn the group members, I hobbled my own ability to focus on my magic and erect a shield. Whispering in Rick's ear to try and avoid them hearing, I whispered a plan that would allow me to protect us. In the end it worked, with Evan's injury the worst but far from life threatening. With his wolf healing, the gashes had stopped bleeding by the time I managed to get a protective bubble around us.

Everyone not carrying the stretcher, besides Rick of course, shifted to their animals, all wolves except our resident bear. Their senses were far keener in that form and many of them proved far better fighters that way also. We attempted to keep a swift pace, knowing now that the sooner we arrived at our destination, the safer we would be. We hoped.

The next hour passed in relative peace, although everyone remained on high alert. Vampires didn't give up that easily, and we all just waited for the other shoe to fall. And fall it did.

With no warning whatsoever the ground beneath us bucked and rolled like a wave from the sea. The animals all managed to maintain their balance, but the four of us on two legs went down hard. The stretcher fell to the ground as the two carrying it pitched off the side of the trail when they lost their balance.

Thankfully, we had strapped her body down, although none of us had considered an earthquake as an obstacle. My shield held and nothing managed to physically attack us, but we'd never make it to Rick's former village if we couldn't stay upright. Under my breath, I beseeched the goddess for mercy.

"Please help us. I can't hold the shield and combat the earth at the same time."

We gathered ourselves and started out again. This time, the disruptions were tremors, mere slivers of the power previously upending our path. It made walking a little sketchy, but doable.

We made it to about the halfway point when a sudden and invisible force crashed against my shield. I managed to maintain it, but the raging migraine the attack caused brought me to my knees. Between the pain in my head and the focus on the magic draining me, I could barely use my telepathy to warn Rick.

"Let the shield down then. We will fight it."

I started to shake my head, stopping when stars exploded on the back of my eyelids. "I can't," I whispered, just loud enough for him to hear. "We don't know what's out there. If it's the evil spirit, I won't even have a chance in this condition. It's taking everything I've got to keep this shield up. If I let it down, I may not be able to get it back. I will not willingly expose everybody with us to her horrors."

Every assault against my protective barrier brought fresh waves of pain. My strength kept fading, and I struggled to find a way to save those with me. Desperate, I plunged my hands into the earth, digging past the rocky topsoil to the soft dirt beneath. My fingers wiggled as I quietly murmured to the sanctuary ground itself.

"I do not want these interlopers here any more

than you do. Please, take my remaining magic and send them away. Give us a chance to reach our destination so we can take the next steps of protecting you fully and forcing them out for good."

Seconds passed with no indication that anyone or anything had heard my pleas. Then a searing pain pierced my palm, and it felt as if something had pierced a hole in my very soul. Every ounce of strength leached out of me and into the earth. Once I felt a pain akin to having an ice pick shoved into my brain, I lost consciousness.

My first waking thought was that I had somehow ended up on a boat. The back and forth swaying made me woozy, but the migraine stopped. Raising my eyelids just a little let in a view of the deep blue sky through the treetops. With no memory of what happened, I worried that I'd been kidnapped.

Luckily, that wasn't the case.

"You're awake." Rick's voice rumbled inside his chest, very near to my ear.

Opening my eyes fully, I looked up at him. "How did you know?"

"Your heart rate accelerated."

"You have no idea how glad I am that it's you. For a

moment, I worried I'd been kidnapped, and you guys were all captured or dead."

"Nope. Whatever you did was extremely successful. What did yo do anyways?"

Before I could answer him, a dry cough wracked my chest. "I'm parched," I croaked out. "Could we stop for a water break?"

"Of course, I'm sorry." Turning part way to address the others, he announced we needed to make a stop.

He set me down in slow motion, making sure my legs could support me before removing his support to just his hand under my elbow. I might have been able to stand, but only as well as a newborn giraffe. Actually, I wasn't nearly that steady.

Plopping down on a log directly off the side of the trail, I waited while Rick handed me a bottle of water. Everyone else did similarly.

"Where are we?"

"Almost there. Once it became apparent you probably weren't going to bounce up and prance down the trail, we decided it was in our best interest to keep moving. I could feel the bubble had popped with a truly magnificent outward force, so I didn't know how long we'd have before something else attacked."

Pulling up my hand, I inspected the sight of the pain. A small pink scar near my crescent mark was the only indication that I'd sacrificed my blood to the earth in exchange for the protection of the forest.

With vague memories my only guide, I explained what I had done to Rick. He frowned when I got to the part about bargaining with my magic, but didn't scold me.

"I didn't know what else to do. That shield only had so much juice left in it, and if I passed out with securing some sort of defense, there's no telling what may have happened to you guys. I couldn't take that risk."

"We should get moving then. We don't know how long this exchange for protection will last. If we maintain a decent pace, we should get there within the next hour, before the sun goes down. Can you walk, or should I carry you for a while longer?"

"I can walk. Probably a little slower than we would like to go, but my reserves are filling back up and I'll be fine."

My knees wobbled and my ankles threatened to throw me to the ground every few steps, but I made it along the trail with faltering progress. Thanks to my weakness, the one hour trek Rick had predicted lasted almost twice as long, but we arrived at his previous home before dark. Walking up on it after it had been mostly abandoned left an eerie feeling in my stomach.

He sent a few of the group out to meet up with the crew sent ahead to inspect the buildings and check the perimeter. We did not want and nasty surprises sneaking up on us. Strangely enough, it didn't seem to have been touched at all.

Ophelia's stretcher got deposited in Rick's former dwelling. He insisted that it could be secured most easily out of them all and would prevent anything from happening to her. While the wolves on patrol did their job, one of the other men set up the central campfire and began preparing dinner.

My expenditures of energy throughout the day left me both exhausted and ravenous. I required some sort of sustenance before I would be capable of strengthening the original wards around the settlement. And absolutely nothing could convince me to skip that step. We knew the vampires were on to our expedition, and no doubt my grandmother's wicked spirit wanted to prevent our success as well.

Not wanting to seem like a slacker, I attempted to help with something, anything, but got firmly directed to a chair by the fire and told to sit and wait for dinner. Despite my outward false scowl, I thanked them because I knew that I had very little left in the tank and I just might fall over into any chore they assigned me. The forest took advantage of my offer and drained every last morsel of magic out of me.

My magic rebounded far faster than my physical body, and I knew I had enough juice in the tank to protect our group overnight, but that would be it. I had no choice but to sleep overnight and make my way to the altar cave the next day. I didn't possess the stamina to do another major magical session the same day.

As much as I felt guilt for my choice, I had been practicing accepting my limitations and reminding myself that I didn't do any of us any good if I ran myself into the ground. At that point, I turned myself into a liability instead of an asset, and my team didn't deserve that. They needed me to help them, not hinder them.

Rick walked over carrying two bowls of a delicious smelling stew and took the chair next to me. Taking the bowl, I thanked him and began shoveling food into my mouth. It seemed calories, and a lot of them, made for the quickest recovery after abusing my magical limits. It didn't cure the exhaustion, but it gave me the physical strength to do what needed to get done, for which I was extremely thankful.

A lone howl filled the air from somewhere far deeper in the forest. The others turned in its general direction, but didn't get up. The wards previously set here would alert us if the boundaries were crossed, so even if someone or something entered the protected space, we would know about it.

Rick provided me a refill of the stew before I needed to ask, and halfway through it I was full and sleepy. Luckily, the wards around the clearing all gathered their power from rune covered stones in Rick's cabin. Once he finished eating, he led me to them.

Fatigue drew out the process of deciphering them in order to know how to best bolster them, but I managed. The group previously agreed that Rick and I would stay in his cabin with Ophelia and the others who did not have patrol duty would divide themselves up against the other three closest options.

Sitting on the couch, I let my head fall back on the back of it. I closed my eyes and prepared to doze off right there.

"Hey, get yourself up and go to the bedroom before you let yourself fall asleep."

"I'm not taking your bed. Besides, I am so tired it will be nothing to sleep right here. *You* should go to bed."

"Nope. You are the one who will be doing the majority of the heavy lifting tomorrow. Your magic will need to be on top of its game, which means your body needs a good night's rest. We don't want to have to put the ritual off for another day because you don't have enough strength to do it due to lack of sleep."

"Ouch, hit me where it hurts why don't you?"

"You know I'm right. Now stop arguing and go to bed."

Struggling to get to my feet, I stumbled through the doorway and pulled the covers back. Unsure if I even kicked off my shoes, I passed out within seconds of my head hitting the pillow. I hung onto wakefulness just long enough to send my thanks out for the help I received earlier in the day and to ask for the same protection to last through the night. After that, my consciousness dropped away, and I slept.

CHAPTER TEN

Dreams did not invade my sleep, but I woke feeling as if I hadn't rested. My thoughts rattled around in my head, jumbled and incoherent. The sun had not yet risen high enough in the sky to shine through the trees and into the cabin windows, so I lay in bed contemplating what I needed to do that day.

Nobody here with us could help me. I was the only magic wielder in the group. My only hope would be to beg the goddess for guidance and assistance if I ran into trouble.

Somehow, I needed to find the instructions in the ransacked cave before I could begin to prepare for the ritual. Then I needed to be sure I had everything I needed, because even though I brought what I "thought" I might need, I'd never seen a spell such as this one and it would be my luck that it called for a pangolin scale and the urine of a platypus.

A yawn escaped me, and I contemplated closing my eyes and trying to go back to sleep. As usual, though, time wasn't on my side. I would most likely need every hour of daylight to prepare for what I assumed would be a midnight ritual.

Before long, the scent of coffee wafted through the slightly ajar door and drove me to get out of bed. Rick looked as if he woke up quite a while earlier. Breakfast would be cooked on the fire pit out front for the entire group, but Rick knew I needed my coffee before I was fit to mingle with any other life forms.

"When do you want to head up to the cave?" He handed me my mug before asking the question.

"Pretty much as soon we're done eating, if that works for you? I know it needs a lot of cleaning up, and I have to search for the spell instructions. The book told me it's in there, but not where."

"It certainly needs more cleaning, but we attempted to put things to right and remove the majority of the debris."

"Oh, goodness..."

"Where is the debris now?"

"Piled just outside of the cave for now. Why do you ask?" His quizzical expression met my panicked one.

"What if the instructions were on pieces of the debris that you cleared away? If it got disposed of, we might never find it!"

"Hmm. Well, even though we removed it from the cave, I am fairly certain that none of the pieces were moved to any other area."

Despite his positive news, the situation was too dire for me to relax until I had the instructions in my possession. Once I held them in my hands and laid eyes on the spell itself, I might relax some. In all seriousness, I would be wound tighter than a spring until Ophelia stood before me and I could hug her tight and get one from her in return. Then I needed to be sure she forgave me for what I had done to her.

Once I'd finished my first cup and gotten a refill, we headed outside to join the others and see if we could help at all with breakfast preparations. Nobody wanted my assistance, so I settled myself into a chair at the fireside and made conversation.

None of the other group members were female, solely because Rick and Isaiah chose the biggest and meanest fighters from the pack to see us to our destination, which made me feel a little lonely. They each made sure I felt welcome. It just made for a different dynamic when you were the only girl.

It also colored any aspect of companionship when their only role for this escapade required that they protect me at all costs. Without me, Ophelia could never come back to us. Without me, there would be nobody left to fight the evil spirit. Without me, the entire pack would be decimated.

The pressure sometimes felt like an elephant taking a seat on my chest. It hit me suddenly and all the air whooshed out of my lungs, sometimes so quickly I saw stars. It made me struggle to take a breath or form any logical thought. I wanted to run away and hide until it was all over, but I knew if I ran away that would be the instant it was over for them and my sinister grandmother's spirit would hunt me down after acquiring enough magic to ensure I didn't have a snowballs chance in hell of beating her.

My pensive thoughts carried me along until Rick drug my attention back to the present.

"Earth to Leah? Hello?"

"Ugh. Sorry. I let me thoughts run away with me and the rabbit hole I fell down was less pleasant than any wonderland I imagined before. What do you need?"

"We're all done with breakfast. Are you ready to go?"

"Sure, just let me help clean up since nobody let me help cook."

He shook his head. "When will you learn, girl? You have bigger priorities than dishes. Everyone knows it and is willing to take on the chores so you can fulfill them."

"I'm sorry, I just feel bad."

"You'll feel worse if Ophelia is sentenced to an eternity of purgatory. Let's go."

Ouch. Talk about pouring an ocean's worth of salt into a raw, open wound. Once again, though, he wasn't wrong. Imagine Ophelia knowing I elected to do a load of dishes rather than save her soul. She'd probably haunt me for my entire life. Then when I died, she'd find my soul and drag me there with her. Okay, so she most likely wouldn't, but I'd still be drowning in guilt for the rest of forever.

Two of the other group members hiked up the trail with us to help with the physical labor. They'd offered to help me look for the spell, but I didn't know how to tell them what to look for since I didn't even know myself. The grimoire might tell me more once in the cave with the appropriate magic, but again, I didn't know. Most of the time, I felt like I didn't know a damn thing.

At the mouth of the cave, we stopped. The vines had grown out of control, making it hard to identify the actual hole in the mountain wall that served as the door. Rick wanted us to find the entrance carefully so as to leave as much foliage hiding it as possible. It meant that we just stuck our arms through the leaves and felt for a break in the stone.

It took only a few minutes, and I gently peeled back the plants to reveal the darkened cave. With lights called up to give us visibility, we surveyed the damage. Rick had said they moved some of the loose stone out, but I couldn't see how. The entire place still had rubble everywhere. It looked like more rubble lay across the floor than had been in the cave originally. The only clear space was around the now shattered altar.

My steps were careful as I moved a few feet into the disaster. I needed to nudge rocks out of my way to locate a safe place to plant each foot. My heart hurt at the destruction of the altar's temple. Making my way to it, I knelt at the base and whispered my prayers.

"I'm going to do my best to repair this damage. I'm not sure how, but I will. I know I need to use the magic that comes from my crescent mark and not from anywhere else, so if you'd like to lend me any suggestions, I'll be happy to follow them."

At the time, no response came forth, but I held onto the faith that she wanted her sanctuary restored and would give me signs when the time was right. After my prayer to the goddess, I took a deep breath and again asked the earth for its help and protection.

"I want to heal the wounds you have suffered and soften the blows they have dealt you. I'm willing to do whatever you need, so long as you show me what must be done."

This time, a gentle rumble rolled through the cave floor. A number of precariously balanced rocks toppled over, but it placed nobody in any danger.

"Thank you."

Turning to Rick, I explained my plan. "I don't know

what I need to do at this point, so for a minute I am just going to sit in here and meditate. I'm hoping if I open my senses and I might be able to find a starting point at least."

"Okay. I'll stand here in the doorway to keep an eye on you, and everyone else will wait outside until you're ready."

Thanking him, I settled in a cross-legged position directly on the cave floor, pushing aside a few of the bigger stones in the area. Both palms rested flat against the earthen floor. My eyes closed, and I tried to "look" at the cave through the magic that flowed through my birthmark. The first few attempts, I found it difficult to siphon out the spirit magic and push it aside, but I managed eventually.

The silvers, purples and blues that were the natural aura had turned murky and dull instead of sparkly and shiny. Streaks of crimson ran through it like rivers of blood. The area directly around the altar circle looked as if it had been shrouded in a dark fog. Thrumming through the air, I felt a throbbing ache, as if the space truly was in pain.

Reaching for it in a metaphysical way I tried to draw it to me so I could cast it out, but it sank deep into the essence and anchored firmly. Reaching back into my memory, since I no longer had my family's grimoires, I tried to recall spells for cleansing and healing.

With a couple of the more intricate ones, I did notice a lightening of the red streaks, but they didn't disappear completely. I had no way of knowing whether it was because I didn't remember them correctly or because they simply weren't strong enough to do the job against such potent destruction. I worked at it for a couple of hours before needing a break.

Rick and I stepped outside, and I sat up against one of boulders in the clearing. We dug snacks and water bottles out of the backpacks and discussed our options. Not far from us, the others sifted through the rubble that had been removed from the cave, looking for any sign of something significant. I offered them snacks, but they declined, telling me they'd taken their break an hour ago.

"I've done what I can for now to try and heal some of the damage. It's less, but not gone. I just don't have the spells needed right now to cleanse it completely."

"We'll get there. Do you know what you need to do next?"

"It's time to ask for more help. If I get any, I will

obviously follow the instructions. If not, I'm going to consult Ophelia's grimoires. If that fails too then I am just going to start looking for anything that might be a clue."

"Sounds like as good a plan as any to me. I wish I had more advice to offer you. I'm sorry I can't be much help at this stage of the game."

"Stop it. You've been so much help already. We each have our roles to play, and this one is mine." I paused and decided to go ahead with my question. "Have you heard from Isaiah? Is there any news about Shelby?"

He looked defeated. "I'm sorry, no. They're looking everywhere for her, but they have to be cautious and look in groups so that nobody else is kidnapped during the search."

"I wish I could go look for her."

"We're going to find her. I refuse to let myself believe otherwise."

Without warning, a rolling pain ran from the top of my head to my toes. The world tipped sideways wand left me briefly, unable to speak. Rick must have noticed and reached out to grab my arm.

"What's happening?"

"An attack. Someone is trying mightily to break through the wards. We need to get down there. Warn the others."

Rick sent out his warning and pulled me to my feet, sending the others to race down the trail ahead of us to help while he steadied me and kept me on my feet whenever a wave of pain threatened to drive me to my knees.

The wards remained intact when we reached the bottom but the spirits unearthly blue light eerily tinted the shimmering spell. She tried to speak to me, but I needed to maintain focus to not pass out from the pain, and wasn't going to let down my mental shields for anything. I'd been practicing for too long to keep her out of my thoughts.

Refusing to let her see me fall, I settled down on the ground, cross-legged once more, and focused on my meditation. The two distinct magics running through me each possessed different traits. I did my best to wind them together, pulling the strengths from both to protect our group and drive her away.

Intent on keeping her out, I didn't notice Rick trying to get my attention until he put his hand on my arm. I opened my eyes and met his.

"She says she wants to talk to you about Shelby."

CHAPTER ELEVEN

Opening my eyes, I looked up at him while struggling to maintain the only thing shielding us from her. "Damn it. She has Shelby?"

"Or knows something about who does."

Distaste turned my expression into a frown. The last thing I wanted to do was converse with the evil bitch. But she knew I wouldn't sacrifice Shelby. She had to know that or she never would have kidnapped her. Letting out a huff, I told Rick my plan.

"I will not let down the wards, but I am going to

open up my mental safeguards just enough to talk to her. I need to keep her out of my head, so please don't interrupt me unless it is a dire emergency. With my efforts split, it will take everything I have to shove her back out again, and she doesn't need to know what I know."

Nodding his understanding, he put his hand on mine. "If you can draw from other's strength, you are welcome to use mine."

"Thanks, but I am going to try not to. Only if there is no other way. I don't want anyone to be weakened if we have to fight."

He settled next to me. "I'll be right here."

I took two deep breaths, focusing on the 'in through your nose and out through your mouth' process, to center myself. In my head, I pictured the block as a huge metal door. Impenetrable. No way in without me opening it.

Then the imaginary me took a long minute and installed every sort of fortifying lock I could come up with. A chain, to ensure the door couldn't open more than a crack. A stopper to brace the door at the bottom so that she couldn't force her way through. Next, I imagined that even if she did get through the door; it led nowhere other that a teeny tiny room, barely big enough to stand in. She might fight her way through, but I kept the "room" utterly empty.

Certain I had secured my psyche from intrusion as completely as possible, I reached out to her.

"What do you want?"

Her evil snicker floated through my head. "I believe it is I who have something *you* want. The question is, how badly do you want to save her?"

"Where is she? What have you done with Shelby?"

Once more, she laughed. It sounded rather like a childish giggle, and if I didn't know better, I never would guess that it belonged to a long dead spirit, and such an awful one at that.

Refusing to engage with her, I let the silence stretch out as I waited for her to answer me. My refusal to pander to her position infuriated her, and she spat the next words at me, her tone full of venom.

"This is not a gift. You will need to give me something in return."

"Technically, you stole her. We are not trading trinkets, and this is not a game. You are giving back something that doesn't belong to you, that you have no right to possess in the first place."

"You for her. That's all I ask. I will return her to her home, and that will be the end of it."

"Absolutely not. I get that you're afraid of me, but I'm not stupid. I don't even know if she is still alive."

"Oh, she is. My friends find her to be quite tasteful."

The image floated into my head. Poor Shelby shackled to a wall. Bruises and puncture marks covered her. One of the dark hair vampires fed from her as I watched. My anger bubbled up like lava during an eruption.

"You let her go. Now."

"Come and get her if you want her that badly."

Before I got the chance to say anything else, her presence disappeared. The metal door in my brain slammed shut, and I locked it securely before turning my attention to Rick, tears flowing.

"She is letting the vampires suck her blood! My friend is chained to the wall being bled dry, and I chose not to save her."

The guilt made it hard to keep down the food I'd been eating at the cave.

"How could you have saved her?" Rick's tone told me the question didn't really require an answer. "Do you really think, no matter what you do, that she would just release her and let her walk away?"

"She said I had to trade myself for her. I said no!" I wailed the last word.

"As you should have. You are the only person who is in her way right now, and she knows that. You cannot let her get her hands on you. You will die, and the rest of us will follow right behind. You know that."

"But what if she dies? What if they tell her I had the chance to save her, and I chose not to?"

"Leah. Shelby knows you better than that. In fact, Shelby would be so angry if you gave yourself up for her. She has friends and family here who will also die if you are captured. People she loves and would gladly sacrifice herself for. She'd do anything to keep them from suffering what she is going through. And if the spirit knows you want her, and if there is even a chance, you might come for her, they will keep her alive."

"But at what cost? I can't imagine her pain right now. Her fear. They're literally eating her alive."

"Then we need to get back to work. The sooner we get these things straightened out, the sooner we can rescue her. Because we will have the strength to do so."

He pulled me to my feet, intent on keeping me from dwelling on the situation. Without even asking, he began to lead me back up the trail to the cave.

"Can you tell Isaiah, please? There is no point of them being out looking for her and risking themselves." I sent out a silent apology to Shelby, knowing that what Rick said made sense.

The path back up the hillside was quiet. Rick conversed with Isaiah, and I tried to use the time to center myself and drive out the fear and anger I felt. If I wanted my magic to guide me, I needed to be calm and open to hearing what it had to say. Focusing on my emotions would only increase the chance I might miss something that the universe presented to me.

We stopped just outside the cave entrance. "Isaiah is pulling all the teams back in, and they will wait until they hear from me before taking any other steps. Everyone has been advised to stay well within the village and not be alone if possible. I don't know if there is anything else we can do right now aside from being exceptionally cautious."

"I think you're right. They need to be careful, and we need to find this spell."

Pushing the vines aside once more, I entered the cavity in the mountain wall and took a minute to look around and really see what there was to see inside. If I couldn't use magic to find the clue, then each piece of rubble would need to be examined and moved outside, kept separate from the other pile that I hadn't even had a chance to look at yet.

Placing my hand on the wall, I made a circuit of the entire room, leaving myself aware of my physical body only enough to ensure I didn't trip and fall. My goal wasn't to learn anything at that point, just to soothe the space. The air hung heavy and dense, a stark change from the original atmosphere.

After doing the entire perimeter, I moved inward, showing the same attention to the interior space. By the time I'd covered all the ground, I felt my connection to the space strengthened. It responded to my ministrations.

Intent on reconnecting the space to the goddess's magic, I finished clearing the center where the altar had stood. Every stone that had not once been a piece of the altar got moved to the outer circle. Even the legs were placed aside, seeing as how I couldn't balance dozens of shards on two legs, one of which lay broken into multiple pieces itself.

Movements slow, I recreated the altar on the ground, putting the pieces back together like a puzzle.

The work took a long time, but in the end eighty-five percent or so of the tableau it had once been could be recognized. Any of the smaller slices that did not fit in an exact place were placed on the largest center piece to keep the entire thing together.

Once satisfied I'd the best that I could, I moved to the next ring. Each one used specific stones to mark its boundaries, and I spent much of my time finding the right ones to create the circle. While not completely understanding the need for the layout, I knew each element had its purpose.

Rick poked his head in. "How's it going in here?"

Pushing my sweaty hair back off my face, I waved him in. "I'm getting there. I feel pulled to set it to rights as best I can before beginning to look for my information, so that's what I'm doing."

"I can't believe how much work you have done in just a couple of hours! It's recognizable again, or most of it anyways. Did you want to go down and have an early dinner?"

"You go ahead. I want to keep pushing forward until I can't any more. It already looks like we won't even be able to begin looking until tomorrow, which means tomorrow night will be the earliest we could perform the ritual, and I don't want to waste any time."

"I don't feel all that comfortable leaving you here by yourself."

"I think this is the safest place I could possibly be, except for maybe at home. You are within screaming distance and I can always reach you the other way, too. Our connection works fine. You can send someone back to check on me in a little while if it makes you feel better."

He winked at me and lifted his hand in a wave. "You're not wrong. Far be it from me to argue with the lady in charge. If you don't come back down by the time the food finishes cooking, I'll bring dinner for you when I'm done eating. Deal?"

"Sounds like a good deal to me. See you later."

Before his shadow even disappeared from the doorway, I lost myself in the work I'd been doing before he arrived. While physically demanding, it somehow felt relaxing and just right. If I asked something of the earth and the spirit, then I wanted to show them I wasn't afraid to give something in return.

Numerous crystals shattered during the assault on the cave, and I had no way of repairing them. Instead, I collected what I could and piled like colors together, trying to keep them in their original groupings.

Needing a break, I slid down against the wall where I'd been sweeping crystals into mounds on the dirt. Resting my head against the cool stone, I threaded my fingers into the dirt on the floor and let it sift through my fingers. The repetitive motion soothed my thoughts, lulling me into a sense of safety and relaxation. I let my eyes drift closed.

While continuing the motions with my hands, I opened my mind to the possibility of communing with the goddess. My steel barrier to keep the evil spirit out had been built solely to withstand an assault from her and didn't get in the way of allowing the goddess in. Not that I held myself in such high esteem that I'd actually be able to keep her out if she truly wanted in. Goddess level was way above my pay grade.

Instead of the white mist of the dreamscape that I'd become accustomed to, I found myself wandering through a stone labyrinth. The walls of the maze held paintings and etchings of symbols from a time long past, most of which didn't look remotely familiar to me. No sounds could be heard. Even my footsteps were swallowed by the silence within.

Endless walking led me nowhere. No matter which

path I chose, or which way I turned, I never reached an entrance or an exit. Slowing, I ran my fingertips over the indents, creating some of the symbols. I tried to feel them with my magic, but they seemed empty. At some point, I became aware of the sound of water dripping.

Instead of trying to follow it, I opened myself to just listening. I focused on each "plop" as the water hit whatever surface it landed on. I noted the amount of time between each tiny splash, aware that the droplets landed on other water or a wet surface.

So engrossed in the sounds I heard, it didn't occur to me to watch where I walked and a single footstep later; I realized too late that no more stone existed. My foot traveled downward and continued on after I should have reached the floor, throwing me off balance and into a darkness that swallowed me up.

CHAPTER TWELVE

The fall seemed to take forever. As the wind rushed by my ears, the sound almost deafened me. I didn't even know if I screamed because I couldn't hear myself. Occasionally my out flung arms brushed against the craggy walls of the hole, bruising and tearing into my skin.

After what felt like hours but was almost certainly only seconds, I hit bottom. Flat on my back, I slammed into the solid stone slab. The breath whooshed out of my lungs like a balloon deflating, and the back of my skull cracked against it. My jaw worked as I attempted to drag some air back into my lungs before my brain shut down from lack of oxygen. I failed, and my eyelids fluttered shut.

Once my body relaxed, it must have begun breathing again as I woke some time later, in the same position but in a great deal more pain than I remembered having before passing out. Cold seeped through the stone and penetrated my bones. Every part of my body stiffened enough that getting up on my own seemed impossible at first. Rolling over onto my stomach brought a wave of dizziness and nausea.

I rested my forehead against my arms, working to find a swath a skin not burning from the cuts and scrapes. What little light I'd been using to see in the maze above no longer glowed, and I couldn't see six inches in front of my face. Praying my magic would manifest itself here, I asked for an orb of light and exhaled in relief when one appeared.

Unfortunately, it didn't do me much good. The orb lit the tiny space around itself, and not much more. Inky blackness stretched outside the space I occupied. Groaning, I tried forcing my body to stand against its will. That third time's a charm phrase is a lie; it took me five attempts to get off my belly and onto my feet, somewhat unsteadily.

Choosing the arm that hurt the least, I put it out in front of me to ensure I didn't run into a wall that stood just outside my scope of light. I shuffled forward until my hand brushed the wall and leaned against it. None of my bones had broken during the fall, but man did every single one of them hurt.

Leaving my hand on the wall, I crept forward, looking for a break in the stone that might indicate a hallway or a way out. The unbroken barrier went on forever. I put one foot in front of the other repeatedly, only to never have my hand meet empty air. Would I ever get out of there? I had no idea where I ended up, or whether I occupied the space physically or only in a dream. If anyone came searching for me, would they find my body still on the floor of the cave, or had I somehow been mysteriously transplanted through time and space to where I thought I was?

Tired and sore, I lowered myself to a seated position on the floor and curled up, pulling my knees against my chest. The dim light from the orb highlighted the injuries to my bare arms, and I winced just looking at them. What a mess. They didn't seem to be healing as quickly as my injuries usually did, either.

After sitting and feeling sorry for myself in the almost-dark and silence for quite some time, my ears began to register a dripping of water once more. While I knew that sound got me to my current situation, following it might be the only way to get *out* as well. After circling what I believed to be the entire wall and feeling nothing wet, I surmised the sound must be coming from somewhere closer to the floor, below where I originally could feel. If It had been dripping from above, I would have been able to feel it at the level I rest my hand on the wall.

Crawling proved somewhat easier as a mode of movement on every part of my body except my knees, and I winced every time the tender spots came down on a pebble or raised area of the uneven floor. Coming to the spot where the water sounded loudest, I paused and began to feel around the wall.

At first, nothing. The sound continued, but I couldn't find the source. Totally on accident, I discovered a tunnel, barely large enough for a person to fit into, if you weren't a large person. The ceiling on the tunnel rose no more than two feet off the floor and the walls barely left room for my shoulders.

Gut instinct said I needed to follow it. Fear prevented me from doing so. If I reached another drop off and fell in, I'd be headfirst, and the fall would likely break my neck. On the other hand, if I didn't, I would be here forever.

"Really?" I asked out loud. "Really? I'm supposed to wiggle my way through a hole in the wall? Where are you taking me?"

Of course, no answer presented itself, just the insistent feeling that this route would take me to where I needed to be. The dimensions of the tight little hallway meant I couldn't even crawl. I had to slither along on my belly if I wanted to follow it.

As best I could, I brushed the pokey stones and debris off to the side with my arms before using my toes to push me forward. Minutes into the excursion, my calves and thighs burned. My toes ached and my arms trembled with the effort to pull my body weight forward. Resting my head on my arms, I closed my eyes briefly to take a break.

Doing so invited every bodily system in me to shut down. Sleep came, if you can sleep during a dream since you are, technically, already asleep. The feeling of overwhelming thirst woke me. My orb of light went out as soon as I stopped using magic to power it, so the passageway remained in total darkness. Even when touching my own nose I couldn't see my hand.

The sound of water seemed louder than I remembered and I wanted nothing more than to find it and get out of there. I'd never been particularly claustrophobic but the tight, dark space wore on my psyche.

As I pushed forward again, I had to stop every few feet to deal with the cramps in my lower limbs. It took everything in me to move forward, so I didn't bother with the orb for light, except every so often just to check my surroundings. At the end of a particularly nasty cramp, my ears registered more water. Not just dripping, but what sounded like waves against the shore. Nothing showed in the orb's reach, so I turned it off and kept scooting forward.

Every so often, I put an arm out as far as I could reach in front of me to check for water. The last thing I needed was to fall face first into an underground body of water. Knowing my luck, I'd be eaten by a water monster. Or simply drown thanks to being so exhausted I couldn't swim.

At long last, my fingertips touched a thin ribbon of

sand. Inching forward, I looked for the water by feel and eventually met the icy cold waves I'd been hearing. Having finally reached what I hoped was my destination, I called on light once more.

The darkness in this cavern didn't mimic the all-encompassing blackness of the previous areas, but as far as the eye could see, in either direction lay an unending ribbon of gray-scaled sand that met an equally unending body of water.

"Oh, for crying out loud. Now what?"

Not expecting a response, I almost jumped out of my skin when a soft voice whispered in my ear, "Swim."

"What?" I jerked my head around to see who spoke, but the beach lay empty. As far as I could see, the only living creature in the area was me.

The fatigue that pulled at my every cell protested even the thought of getting into that water. Even if nothing tried to eat me, I'd most definitely sink to the bottom like a rock. My reserves were empty, and I had nothing more to give.

"You need this." The whisper came again in my ear. This time I didn't bother to look for the source.

"I can't," I whispered.

The voice did not respond. Instead, I looked up just

in time to see a huge wave barreling toward me. I had nowhere to go, even if I could get up and run. If I went back into the tunnel, I would drown.

The water crashed over me seconds after I took the deepest breath my lungs could hold. It drug me out, across the sand and over the rocky seabed. Briefly, I rose to the surface to gulp another breath and went under once more. The process repeated as I got tossed and tumbled within the current. I lost all hold on my magic and prayed I wouldn't rise up into the dark.

At some point, I kicked my way to the surface and found the water to be calm and flat. Turning over onto my back, I spent some time floating, taking deep breaths and trying to recuperate. Now what? My entire journey landed me in the middle of an underground ocean with no idea what to do next.

The salt stung my eyes, confirming that it must be some sort of ocean. Perhaps it was connected to the sea surrounding the peninsula, but I couldn't be sure. Not wanting to swim without being able to see land, I waited. Something had brought me this far. I had to believe whatever or whoever it was would show me where to go next.

The idea that it could be the evil spirit leading me

to my death evaporated. Whatever ran this show had taken care not to drown me in the waves, so I doubted it would bother to kill me now. Floating along, I used the time to ponder my reason for being there.

There had to be a point to this. No fathomable explanation came to me, no matter how hard I tried to find one. Yet, here I languished. No idea which way to land, or back home.

As I ruminated on my situation, a soft, red glow grew brighter. The color reminded me of a sunset or sunrise, but of course where I was had no sun, just a dim light whose origin remained unknown.

"You need this." Again, the voice. The voice without a body.

"I need what?"

What in heaven's name was this person or thing trying to tell me I needed? A bath? As I questioned the premise behind the statement, the red light grew brighter. Within seconds, the light had turned into a laser beam streaking up through the waves and shooting toward the heavens.

"I need to get something down below the water?!"

Testing the water depth, I righted my body to a vertical position and let myself sink a little. The bottom never touched my toes. Great. I'd have to swim down. Maybe it wanted me to drown myself rather than committing murder and drowning me themselves. Tilting my head back to avoid a wave in the face, I took a minute to relax and prepare for my swim.

Taking in a deep breath, I turned and swam toward the ocean floor below. The salty water burned my eyes, making it hard to search for whatever the red light came from. For the first few dives, I didn't even come close to the bottom, let alone to finding whatever I supposedly needed.

"Let me help you."

Barely giving me enough time to grab a lungful of air, a force wrapped around my wrist and drug me down. Keeping my eyes closed, I just held my breath and hoped we'd get to wherever I needed to be before my air ran out. Pressure guided my hand to an item warm and smooth, slightly large than my hand.

My fingers wrapped around it and tugged, but it seemed to be stuck in the sand. My lungs burned. I needed to get to the surface before it was too late. A heavy pull yanked against the stone and I felt it gave way. The force that had been guiding me disappeared, and I turned to head for the surface. Before I could get there stars burst across my vision and I lost consciousness.

CHAPTER THIRTEEN

The first thing to register next was a great pain in my chest and the feeling that I still couldn't breathe. Every breath I tried to take skipped into my lungs and rushed right back out again. On the next exhale, I managed to groan in protest.

"Oh, my goddess! Leah? Are you okay? Can you hear me?"

"Uhumph..."

"Crap. I'm sorry. Are you alright?"

The effort it took to force my eyes open astounded

me. If I could've kept them closed and slept for a month, I would have. Every piece of my body needed the rest. It took my magic to give me enough of a boost to wave him off.

"Stop it." The mumble barely seemed audible to my own ears, but his hands left me and there were no more questions for a minute.

Cracking my eyelids, I tried to figure out my location. Even the dim light burned, but I recognized the altar cave. Had the entire preceding experience really been just a dream? As a muscle cramp wracked my body and my fists clenched in pain, a smooth, hard object entered my awareness. Jerking my arm up, I pried my eyes open to see a red crystal in my fist.

Rick saw me struggling to sit up and offered his assistance. Leaning once more against the cave wall, I stared at the opaque rock. Had this thing been giving off the red laser beam of light at the bottom of the ocean in my dream?

Before I could tell Rick, I leaned to the side and vomited water. A lot of water. Choking and gagging it all out left tears streaming from my eyes.

"Water, not salty," I croaked out. "Please."

He grabbed the backpack from the floor next to him

and rummaged through it, coming up with a partial water bottle. The first sip made me gag, but I managed to keep it down. After another couple of sips, the urge to throw up passed completely, but every breath burned my throat and lungs. My ribs ached and my brain felt fuzzy.

"Are you okay?"

"Maybe?" I wanted to laugh, but it hurt too bad.

"I had the weirdest dream." I couldn't seem to force my voice to any level above a whisper. "Why are you up here? Are you done with dinner already?" Time didn't seem to make sense.

I ran my hands over my face, trying to rub the weariness away, and they came away sticky. Blood stained my palms and the inside of my fingers. No memory of a bloody injury surfaced.

My surprise must have shown on my face, because Rick offered an explanation. "You had a bloody nose when I got here."

"Ah. Okay. Um..."

Finding a way to explain what I just experienced wound up being harder than one would think. My brain just didn't want to work. My mouth couldn't or wouldn't cooperate with the few coherent thoughts my brain did form.

"We need to get you down to a bed to rest. Then you probably need some food and medical attention. I'm going to carry you back."

"No. No, no, no. I need to be here."

"Leah, this time I'm not giving in. You have to recuperate or you will be no good to anyone. Just trying to talk to me made your nose bleed again. Whatever happened, you can tell me about it after we get you taken care of and I am not taking no for an answer. We'll come back."

Leaning over, he scooped me up into his arms and the pain of the movement made me pass out again before we reached the mouth of the cave.

Fragments of the dreamscape slipped in and out of my subconscious. The smell of salty sea air wafted in on a breeze for a single breath, only to be followed by the dank smell of wet stone I remembered from the tunnels. The scrapes and bruises along my arms burned as a reminder of my crawl through the dark, then disappeared as the focus on my aches and pains from the fall intensified.

Blessed blackness crept over the pain to drown it out temporarily, but never stayed as long as I would have liked. Somewhere between dream and subconscious, I floated, never quite making it to wakefulness. Sometimes I thought I heard voices of people I knew and loved, but they faded before I could identify them.

Not once did I see, hear, or feel my grandmother's spirit. While the pain made itself known, I felt no fear. The worry that I was missing something important hovered in the background, but not in a way to make me panic. If the pain would heal and subside, I'd be happy to float suspended the in-between for a long, long time.

"Leah. Le-ah. Can you hear me?"

A voice intruded into one of my blissful dark periods, and I didn't want to acknowledge it. The interruption aggravated me. Why couldn't they just let me sleep? Not forever, just until nothing hurt anymore. That shouldn't be too much to ask.

"Leah!"

"Ugh... What do you want?" What I'd intended to come out as a snap ended up more of a croak, the words dragging against the sides of my throat like a hot fire poker.

My throat felt dry from disuse and my eyes didn't seem to want to open despite the instructions from my brain to do so. Swallowing a couple of times helped my throat, but my brain just wanted to go back to sleep.

"Oh shit, Leah, thank the goddess." Isaiah's voice penetrated the fog in my brain.

"What... why..?" I huffed. "Why are you here?" My voice upgraded from a croak to a whisper, but at least these words didn't hurt me to say like the first set.

"Look at me, please." The urgency in his voice prodded me to try and comply.

Turning my head in the direction his voice came from brought a groan crawling up out of my mouth. None of my muscles wanted to be moving. Squeezing my eyes shut tighter first, I tried again to open them. They obeyed, somewhat begrudgingly. Even with my eyelids raised, my vision lacked clarity. Blinking helped, but not as quickly as I would have liked. It just seemed like my eyelids were spreading gritty sand all over my corneas.

His hand took mine, and he leaned in close. "I was so worried about you."

"I'm fine. You didn't need to come all the way up here."

"You are anything but fine. We thought the spirit might have gotten to you and we'd lost you for good."

His statement got me to open my eyes and really

look at him. "Overdramatic, much?"

"Leah, honey. You've been out cold for three days. You've had random nose bleeds for no reason. Your wounds are not healing like they should be. We've had valid cause to be worried. Very worried. Rick is coming to see you now that you're awake. He's been beside himself."

"I'm sorry, what? Three days? I need to get back to the cave."

"Absolutely not. Right now, you aren't going anywhere."

"You can't tell me what to do!" Already he made my nerves sing.

"You're right, I can't. But in your current condition, I doubt you can even get out of the bed by yourself and there isn't a soul here who is going to help you before we're certain you're better."

Glaring, I did my best to swing my legs over the side of the bed and sit up. One leg did make off the bed, but the motion triggered a charlie horse that brought me to tears.

"OW. My butt cheek is being tied in a knot. It hurts. It hurts so bad!"

The muscle had cramped so badly that I couldn't

even get my leg back into the bed without help. I stared at him with tears running down my cheeks as he gently lifted me back into the bed and tucked the blanket back around me. I closed my eyes against the discomfort and tried to breathe through it as I dug my fist into the muscle in an attempt to release it.

By the time I opened my eyes again, Rick stood next to Isaiah at the side of the bed, just watching me.

"You okay?"

"I think I'd rather die than do that again," I whispered.

He chuckled. "I highly doubt that. It was just a cramp. You shouldn't have tried to get out of bed so quickly or so soon. Those muscles have been unused for days at this point."

"Which is why I *need* to get up. We don't have days to spare. I need to find that ritual and save Ophelia's soul."

"Yes, we do. But not at the expense of your life."

The next tears to fall from my eyes were driven by emotion, not physical pain. I could not fail her. I'd never forgive myself if I did.

"I owe her. Even if it costs me my life. I kidnapped her soul!"

"Leah, don't get too worked up, your-" Isaiah paused.

Before he finished the sentence, I felt a sticky warmth leak from my nostril and run downward toward my lip. Using my thumb, I wiped it away and stared at the offensive crimson liquid smeared across the pad, filling in the whorls of my fingerprint.

Rick handed over a tissue so I could wipe up. Thanking him, I held it to my nose and tilted my face to the ceiling.

"Okay, let's dial it back a little here. We will get the ritual and you will reunite her soul with her body. But you have to be running at optimal levels to perform that kind of magic. It is going to take a lot out of you and you need to be ready for it. If you keep pushing yourself now, you won't heal and won't be able to pull it off."

Isaiah leaned closer, took a sideways look at Rick, and asked a question. "Can you tell us what even happened to you?"

Nodding, I let out a deep breath. Including as many details as I could remember, I led them through the sequence of events that wound up with me floating in the middle of an underground sea.

"Oh! The crystal. A red one! Did you see it when you

came to get me?" Panic set in at the thought that I'd gone through all of that torture for nothing.

Rich walked over to the dresser and picked something up off the top. "This?" He held aloft the ruby-like stone.

I heaved a sigh of relief. "Yes. May I see it, please?"

As I inspected it, I finished telling them how I came to find it, and how I came to be passed out in the cave after my ordeal. The contours of the stone looked similar to the crystals that formed naturally in the cavern around the altar.

Turning it over and over in my hands, I let them ask their questions and answered them the best I could. Yes, I knew I was dreaming. No, I didn't know who brought me there. No, I didn't feel like I was in danger. Yes, I think whoever led me was trying to help me.

"I think this is my answer. The compass, if you will, to finding the information I need to find in the cave. It didn't come with instructions, but I know I can figure it out. In the ocean it was glowing so brightly, and the light is what I saw first."

Rick let me know that some of the others were preparing lunch so that I'd be able to eat soon and hopefully start to regain my strength. Food sounded delicious. Getting out of this bed and back to searching the cavern sounded even better.

As much as I hated to admit it, I knew that my body did need to recover. Unable to believe that I needed three days just to wake up, I prayed it wouldn't be three more before I could get out of bed. We didn't have that kind of time to waste. Our days were numbered, and the minutes were running by like sand through an hourglass.

Isaiah planned to stay here and help me work in the cave, since we had decided it was too risky for anyone to go looking for Shelby. Nobody else had heard anything, and I cried again, thinking about how scared she must be. While we waited for lunch, we talked about the best ways to protect everyone else in the pack, and how we could find out more about those who were still missing. Until we had proof, each of us wanted to treat those who were gone as if they were still alive and this was a rescue mission.

As we discussed the possibilities, I noticed my eyes start to feel heavy. Before I even got some food in me, the conversation drained what little energy I mustered upon waking, and I drifted off once more into a dreamless sleep.

CHAPTER FOURTEEN

My brain registered the smell of food before it woke fully. Isaiah came through the door with a bowl of something that smelled divine. Of course, when you haven't eaten in days, I expect just about anything would smell delectable. He smiled when he saw my eyes open.

"I expected this might rouse you. Hungry?"

"Starved." I couldn't help but grin. "How long have I been asleep this time?"

"Only about an hour. Let me help you sit up."

He set the food on the nightstand and situated me against the headboard and some pillows so I could eat. It hurt and everything in my body still ached, but not like the type that caused me to pass out when Rick brought me down from the cave.

It took me about five minutes to inhale the first bowl of stew, and Isaiah stepped out to bring me another. Letting the food settle while I waited, I ruminated on the crystal. Someone or something deemed it very important I have it, pulling me across space and time to take me to it and make sure I got it, even at the risk of my life. Whether it would help me discover the ritual in the cave, or be useful for something else entirely, I didn't yet know. At the moment, I prayed it was the former. Once I had Ophelia back to help me, things would move along much quicker.

Rick came in with my second bowl. "Isaiah had to do something real quick. Said he'd be in after a few minutes. He asked me to bring the food in though because he thought you might start eating the furniture if I didn't!"

Chuckling, I didn't argue. "He might be right. The first bowl calmed the hunger pains some, but I'm still ravenous."

As I ate, I watched Rick watching me. His face scrunched up in thought, but he didn't say anything.

"Why are you looking at me like that?"

He sighed. "Leah, you almost died. When I got up to the cave, you weren't breathing. Your lips were blue and your nose had been gushing blood, although it was stopped, I think. I had to do CPR. Then you vomited up a bunch of water."

"I really almost drowned, didn't I? I knew I was in the dream, but I kept hoping it would be just like a regular one and when the bad thing happened, I would wake up. Thank you for coming to find me. I'd be dead if it weren't for you."

"I'm glad you're still here, kid. If not, I don't know what we'd do. I hope that crystal was worth it."

"I'm not sure what it's for yet. But, since I don't think the whole dream thing was the spirit trying to kill me, I believe whoever it was, maybe the goddess herself, was trying to help. Otherwise, why make sure I got the crystal? I could have been killed a dozen different ways in those tunnels. And I wasn't."

"I think you're right. It just worries me. We can't even let you sleep without worrying that something could happen. We might have to take shifts watching you nap so that someone will notice if you stop breathing."

"Ew. No. That's creepy. If I knew someone was watching me, I'd never be able to fall asleep. And once we are done here, I'll go back to the house. It's protected there and hopefully I can get my rest without fearing for my life."

"I hope so. Stubborn girl."

"I need to get out of this bed and up to the cave."

Instead of arguing with me, he let out an exasperated exhale and held out his arm to help me to my feet. Swinging my legs over the bed pulled at the muscles that hadn't been used for a while, but no more cramps plagued me. Getting to a standing position made me disoriented at first, and I needed a minute to collect my bearings. Even after I felt steady enough to walk, I still needed his support to move out of the room and toward the front door.

By the time I was making my way out the front door, Isaiah was making his way in. His mouth opened at the same time my hand went up.

"Shh. Not a word. Help me or get out of my way."

He looked at Rick, who shook his head. "As much as

I would like her to rest more, she has a point. We have very little time to get this done."

Isaiah huffed. "Okay. When all of this is over, I expect you to stay in bed for a week."

I snorted. "I will if you do."

The three of us made our way back to the cave, my dreamscape prize clenched tightly in my fist. If I almost died for the stupid thing, I'd be damned if I lost it before I got to use it.

The vines still hung off to the side, since Rick hadn't bothered to stop and pull them back in place as he rushed to get me back to the cabin. Lighting it up with orbs, I took a minute to look around and see if anything jumped out at me. Of course, nothing did.

As I worked at righting the cavern, I'd placed the altar back where it belonged, as well as numerous pedestals and podiums. Some of the statuary once gracing the pedestals had been shattered beyond repair and I prayed one of them wouldn't wind up being the one I needed.

Holding the crystal high in the center of the room, I tried to make it light up the way it had been in the ocean. In my imagination, the little beam of light turned on like a flashlight and pointed me precisely to what I needed. Of course, my imagination did little to influence real life, and nothing happened. Not even a shimmer.

Rick and Isaiah offered suggestions randomly as things popped into their mind, but none of us seemed to know what to do.

"What if it has to be done at night?"

Isaiah glanced backward out the cave door. "Well, then we'll know soon because the sun is already going down."

My stomach clenched. Time kept slipping away. We'd already been at the village here for longer than I had planned to take to get everything done that needed to be and we barely got started yet. The sky outside got darker and nothing changed inside the cave. Even after turning the orbs off, the crystal gave off no light.

"I need help. Without it, I can't do this."

"We're helping you as best we can, Leah." Isaiah sounded terse.

"Not from you, although I appreciate it. I am going to see if I can ask the goddess to show me the way to use it."

Shooing them off to the side, I took my place in the center near the altar pieces. Sitting in a loose butterfly pose, I placed the crystal in the dirt between my legs, propped against my heels. In order to reach her, I closed off my physical mind and opened up my psyche as far as I dared without leaving myself vulnerable to an attack of any kind.

The air in the cavern hummed at a low vibration. Nothing more could be heard. It thrummed up through the floor and rose from my hips to the top of my head. In silence, I meditated, waiting to receive a message of any kind. Just as my legs grew tingly and numb from the position, the crystal began to warm against my heels.

Not wanting to open my eyes and break the spell if it was too early, I continued as I had been, hoping I would somehow know when the right time would be.

"Leah. Look." Rick's whisper barely reached my ears.

Opening my right eye ever so slightly, I could see that the crystal was now emitting a very faint light. It illuminated the single beam of moonlight stretching across the floor. The beam ended at the podium in the far corner, directly on an indent in the stone.

What if the crystal was a key? Grabbing it off the floor, I made my way over and tried to fit it in the cutout. After turning it multiple ways, a crack rang out and the two pieces of stone became one. Try as I might, the red stone would no longer budge. If this didn't show me what I needed to know, I'd be screwed because I couldn't force it out without breaking it.

For a long minute, nothing happened. Then the podium itself began to emit a faint glow. Pulling myself to a standing position, I inspected the lectern. The worn stone made it difficult to surmise what might be inscribed on it, but as the light grew brighter, it became clearer.

"Oh! This is the symbol on the front of the grimoire Ophelia left me. I need the book. I need to set it here."

"I'll run back and grab it." Isaiah turned and headed down the hill before letting me say another word.

Rick and I stood close together, watching the moonbeam. I feared if we didn't get the book on it before the moon changed position, our chance for tonight would be lost and we would have to wait another twenty-four hours that we didn't have to spare.

After a minute, I felt Isaiah reaching out for me, asking for the location of the grimoire. He left in such a hurry from the cave I didn't have a chance to tell him where to find it. Directing him to it took only a second before he informed me he was on his way back.

Isaiah re-entered the cave, not at all out of breath, and book in hand. He passed it to me. Opening it to the page I prayed held the ritual spell I needed, I set it gently on the podium and waited silently, beseeching the goddess in my mind. This had to work. I didn't have any more time to spare.

After tense seconds, the words once more floated to the surface of the page, this time filling it from edge to edge. Unfortunately, the passages weren't written in any sort of language that I recognized.

"Damn it. Do either of you know what language this is?"

Both of them leaned over to peer over my shoulder, then exchanged a look.

"What? Do you or don't you?"

"Leah, we can't see anything at all. It still looks like a blank page to us."

"Oh, for crying out loud. Of course, it isn't as easy as just getting the words on the page. Now I need to figure out *how* to read them."

Squeezing my eyes closed, I pinched the bridge of my nose. After a couple of deep breaths, I rubbed my palms down my cheeks one last time and opened my eyes. Reading couldn't happen with one's eyes closed.

At first, I tried reading them just like I had the ones in Aunt Aimee's attic. Just staring at them for a few minutes and letting them seep into my subconscious. No dice.

Next, I tried using my magic. I tried to translate with it. I tried to change the image on the page to a language I could read. Nothing changed.

Finally, in desperation, I closed off the magic flowing through my crescent mark and fully embraced the spirit magic Ophelia taught me to wield. A breeze ruffled my hair. Though surprised, I managed to ignore it and focus on the task at hand. The characters on the page wavered and swirled, but didn't quite become legible.

Isaiah tried to speak to me, but I cut him off with a wave of my hand. He couldn't interrupt me when I was so close to success. My eyes remained trained on the page.

Desperate, I bit the meaty part of my palm, just below my thumb, and smeared a drop onto the page. Longs seconds passed with nothing happening. My body temperature rose slightly, and the wind rose once more. Once the wind died down, the blood on the page absorbed completely and the alphabet became readable to me.

"Yes." I whispered the word, afraid to do anything to upset the balance I felt was so precarious. The book had chosen to accept me.

"Is it what you need?" Isaiah kept his voice to a whisper as well.

"I need a way to make sure I can copy this. I can't forget anything."

Rick pulled a small wire-bound notebook out of his jacket pocket, along with a pen. "Tell me. I'll write down every single syllable you say."

I read him the page, slowly, from top to bottom. We then went over it a second time to make sure what he wrote matched what I read completely. After we knew we had the words right, I described each illustration on the page and where it went in relation to the paragraphs.

The illustrations led to frustration for both of us until I took the book from him and ripped a couple of pages out. Placing them over the book, I attempted to use more magic to trace a reasonable copy. The results weren't optimal, but got the job done.

After staring at the open book for at least five more minutes, committing it to memory as best I could, I had to force myself to close it. I could only do what I could do, and I had ingredients to gather. The preparation would tax my inexperienced skills, but I had no doubt I could perform the ritual.

Holding the book close to my chest, I looked at the guys. "I think I'm ready to go prepare. I'll need some help to find some items the ritual requires, though."

"Just let us know. We'll get it." Rick was quick to pledge his assistance.

Isaiah nodded in agreement. "Just let us know."

"Can I have a second? I'll meet you outside."

Once they were outside and in the clearing, I sank to my knees. Balancing the book on my lap, I released my crescent mark magic and sent waves of both out into the universe.

"Thank you. I know I couldn't have done this without your help."

Rising, I met the guys at the opening in the cliff wall and helped to arrange the vines back into place. It was time to get to work.

CHAPTER FIFTEEN

The path back down to the cabins passed quickly as we tried to delegate who would do what. Before we could divide up the spell ingredients, we had to go through my backpack to see which of the items I brought with us, which we could find here in the small village and which ones someone would have to travel to procure.

Rick's kitchen turned into my command center, and I spread out the supplies from my backpack. From Rick's notes, I made a list of the items needed for the spell. The backpack stash yielded about fifty percent of what we needed. Not bad for total guess work.

A few of the other items we found around the village. All told we still needed seven specific things to perform the ritual. Three of them I knew for certain were in Aunt Aimee's attic. One of them I thought we could likely find in the basement. That left the other three. Rick agreed to take me to check Ophelia's cabin and see if she had them there. If they weren't, we would have to make plans to go and find them.

Since Ophelia's place required the least travel, we went there first. Her old front porch looked lonely. Not exactly abandoned, although it had been, but just forlorn. The wooden rocking chair sat alone to the left of the door. The drapes on the front windows had been pulled, and it made the front of the house look sad, as if it, too, missed her presence.

We pushed open the door and slipped into the house in silence. Aside from some dust, it looked as if it just sat patiently waiting for her to return. Her things were still exactly as she left them, because she had intended on coming back. Her innate tidiness shone through the dust. Everything placed just so precisely as she liked them.

"I'm just going to stand here and wait for you. I

wouldn't recognize these items if they bit me in the butt, so I'd rather just stay out of your way."

"Okay. I don't blame you. I feel a little bit like I'm intruding on her privacy. I'll be going through everything because I can't even begin to guess her habits."

"I do know she used the bedroom off the dining area as her workspace, if that helps."

"Oh, yes. I'd rather start there than in her bedroom."

We walked through the space and I reached up to open the door, earning myself the shock of a lifetime. I flew back and crashed into the dining table. Cussing, I managed to trip myself trying to get up and knocked the chair into the wall.

"Are you okay?" Rick rushed over to help me up and move the furniture out of my way.

"Fine. Wards. I don't know why on the goddess's green earth it didn't occur to me that she would absolutely have protection set up to keep others out of her workspace."

"Does that mean you can't get in?"

"I probably can. I just need to use my spirit magic to try and unravel them. She began teaching me how to do that before, so I just need to try. I'm most likely rusty and never got super great at it to begin with. Like everything else I've been discovering, there just hasn't been the time for me to practice it."

Reaching out, I slowly advanced until I came into contact with the very edge of the ward. Pulling on the memories of the lessons she gave me, I looked for the pattern in the magic. Seeking out the end of the "string" would help me to unravel it and gain access.

She'd made it hard to find, but I managed. From there, it resembled straightening out a lock of hair that had gotten caught up in one of those kids' toys that had all the little spikes. Strand by strand, they had to be disentangled and set aside. By the time I got the first couple done, sweat poured down my forehead. About three quarters of the way through my nose began bleeding again. I'd be anemic by the time all this was over if it kept doing that.

She made the last line of defense the most complicated and I could feel my legs getting weak as I worked on it. Before they gave out on me and dumped me on the floor, I sat down in the dining chair Rick drug near me. He'd been told not to interrupt me for any reason, but I felt his concern.

As I finished, the ward dropped with zero fanfare and the door swung open on well-oiled hinges. Lights came on automatically as I moved into the doorway. From that vantage point, I took a minute to take in the room and get a feel for it. For all the organization and orderly airs throughout the rest of her life, the workspace was a free for all.

Books and herbs and crystals and dishes of all kinds covered every available space. The shelves had items sticking out every which way, haphazardly stuffed wherever there seemed to be a little room. Some of the herb jars sported labels, others, it was a take your best guess situation. The only free horizontal surface was the worktable in the center of the room.

Aside from the doorway, not a single inch of wall space remained uncovered. Floor to ceiling bookshelves stood edge to edge. In the small spaces about the desk or counter, she tacked papers of all kinds and hung different charms and crystals. I'd never seen any place like it in my life.

Meeting Rick's eyes, I shrugged. "I'm just going to have to dig through everything in here and see if I can locate what we need. Unless you happen to be privy to the way her mind works well enough to tell me the method to her madness?"

"Ha! I'm sorry to say I can't help you. Knowing her though, there is a methodology in there. It's just a matter of whether you could work it out."

"Okie dokie. Search and find it is then."

"Do you want me to help you dig through things?" His expression told me he really wanted me to decline his offer.

"Do you know what you're looking for?"

He shook his head. "No?"

His distaste made me giggle. "Just stand by and keep me company then, huh? I like having someone else here with me. It feels just a little creepy knowing the last time she was in here she was living and now she's not, and it's sort of my fault."

"Oh, Leah. It's not your fault she died. We can blame the wolves who bit her. We can blame the spirit who incited the war. Heck, we can even blame her for getting involved. But her death cannot be blamed on you."

A single tear escaped at his words. "Thanks. I can't help but feel somewhat responsible, though."

As we talked, I began at the workstation nearest the door, since one of the ingredients I needed should be in a bottle. The herb's most common form was to be dried. Thankfully, I knew of it, and had seen it before, so I would be able to recognize it when we ran across it. The same with one of the other items on the list, another crystal.

The last item, though? What a doozy. I'd never heard of it, read about it, or otherwise been exposed to it. I'd be needing a little divine guidance in order to get my hands on it. Hopefully, it could be found here on the peninsula. If we had to leave to get it, we'd be too late. We were on borrowed time already.

This ritual needed to be done right the first time. No such things as second chances when it came to calling a soul back to its body. If the soul did not seat itself correctly, the stasis spell would be nullified and the body would immediately decompose. Once that happened, you couldn't ask the soul to inhabit an unusable vessel.

Before I ran across the herb I started searching for, I hit on a drawer full of various crystals, and much to my surprise, many of them had little labels marking their resting place. Scanning the rows I hoped to find the crystal on my list but and I found an empty space instead.

"Damn it!"

"Problem?" Rick craned his neck to see around me to what I looked at.

"There's a space in here for the crystal I'm looking for, but it's empty."

"Well, at least we know she has one. We just need to find it."

Her penchant for sometimes labeling things helped me out when it came to the herb. An entire bottle sat proudly on the little shelf above the workbench. I handed it to Rick to put in the backpack.

"One down, two to go."

The crystal I searched for hopefully hadn't been removed from the room and taken elsewhere for a ritual or use in some other spell. The sample from the tray didn't measure quite as large as I would have liked, but it still fulfilled the requirement. I just needed to find it.

After what felt like hours of looking, the tiny silver quartz found its way to me. Nestled in the center of a dried floral bloom that I happened to knock off the shelf. The flower hit the desktop and the tiny crystal rolled its way across the wood and make a thunk on the rug covering the floor.

"Ha! There it is!"

Dropping down to my knees, I swept my hand under the edge of the cupboard next to the desk to fish it out from where it rolled upon landing. Rubbing the dust off of it, I cradled it in the palm of my hand. I held it aloft to show Rick.

"We've got it. I'm so glad. I was beginning to think I'd never locate it in all of this stuff."

"I knew you would. The universe is bringing you what you need."

"Now, if only I can find the offering plate I need to use."

We shut her workroom door as we left, and I paused. Something urged me to replace the wards. While they might not be the same as she would put up, they would offer some protection if others came snooping around the mostly abandoned site.

Rick elected to wait outside as I did my final task. Since I'd put up many more wards than I'd taken down, the process didn't leave me as drained as dismantling it had. But on top of my earlier expenditure, my body was feeling the loss of energy reserves and needed sustenance. The trek back to the house still needed to be made to gather what we needed from the attic and the basement room.

Isaiah had food ready and waiting so I could refuel and leave as soon as possible. Exhaustion caught me off guard, and I stumbled slightly while taking a seat at the table.

"Let me go get what you need. You can rest."

"Isaiah, you can't. Only I can get into the sanctuary room in the basement. The door will not only refuse to open for you, you could get hurt. And I can't bear anyone else getting injured. Not on my behalf when I can easily prevent it by doing it myself."

I knew that he knew I had a point when he didn't argue with me.

"How about I carry you, then? You are extremely light and even carrying you we both know I can run faster and farther than you. I can cut the travel time nearly in half."

"I'm sorry? You want to carry me? Like a baby?"

"I was thinking more along the lines of a piggyback. But whatever will make you agree with me will work."

I snorted. While I didn't relish the idea, I conceded he had a point about the speed and travel time. If not afraid of getting stuck, I might have tried to use my wolf form to travel, but I just didn't trust it. That first, and possibly last, time hadn't been confidence inspiring. I'd be a sitting duck stuck in wolf form.

With the backpack hoisted up onto my shoulders, I nodded at him. "Let's do this. The sooner we get what we need, the sooner we can complete the ritual."

He wisely agreed not to gloat and just offered a hand. Pulling me close, he kissed my forehead.

"This won't take long at all."

"Let's just pray that nothing tries to waylay us and we can get there and back quickly." I turned toward Rick. "If it gets dark we will just spend the night at the house and come back here first thing in the morning and we can begin to worry about the dish then."

"Sounds good." He pulled me in for a quick hug. "Stay alert and be safe. It's been a little too quiet for my liking."

"Right?! This seems a little strange. I'm waiting for something to happen."

"Don't speak it into existence. Just keep your eyes open and always be aware of what is going on around you."

"We'll be fine." Isaiah shook Rick's hand. "I'll keep you updated."

With a last wave at the others in the clearing, I climbed up on Isaiah's back and got as situated as possible. I'd be sore by the time we arrived, but wanted to make better time more than I wanted to be comfortable. My arms wrapped loosely around his neck, hoping I didn't choke him, and my legs barely fit around his waist to lock my ankles. He supported me by holding on to the backs of my thighs and took off at a fast jog.

"You doing okay back there?"

"Yep. Just don't leave me behind if I fall off!"

I could feel his body shaking as he tried not to laugh. "As if I would let you fall. Hang tight."

He put on a burst of speed and we wound our way deeper into the woods, headed for the house and most of the remaining ingredients.

CHAPTER SIXTEEN

Only his pounding footsteps interrupted the silence in the woods. We drew close to the babbling stream and then passed it. Dry leaves crunched underfoot every so often, but the thudding of his tennis shoes rarely went unmuffled by the pine needles blanketing the path.

The jostling about made my still tender muscles ache, but not so terribly that I needed him to stop and put me down. I watched the blur of trees as they flew by, marveling at his speed even with my added weight. Resting my head against his back, I pondered the

situation of obtaining the last object required to
perform the ritual.

Over and over I tried to find it in my mind. To recall
if I had seen something like it in all the times I had been
here in my life. Nothing rang a bell, but it's not
something I would have noticed unless really looking for
it anyways. Aunt Aimee could have had something that
would fit the bill sitting on her coffee table at some
point, and I might have looked right past it.

My subconscious took its turn with the problem,
playing with the possibilities. I needed a single offering
plate or dish of all four elements. Earth. Fire. Air. Water.
I didn't even see how such an item could be made. How
do you keep fire in a dish? Especially at the same time as
water?

"Leah."

My own name registered in my ears as I felt myself
sliding down his body. My legs immediately said "no
thank you" and buckled under my weight. If his hands
hadn't been supporting me, I would have found myself
seated on the porch floor.

"We're here already?"

"Yes, sleepyhead. You dozed off, which no doubt
made the trip much shorter than it would have been

otherwise. At least for you." He winked.

"Ha. Keep it up, mister."

The wards recognized me instantly, and the door swung open. The house felt alone and empty. Knowing that out of all our family only I was left made me pause. Our blood line ended here if I didn't have children. If my grandmother succeeded, our entire branch of the family tree would be no more. Maybe that wasn't such a bad thing after all.

Isaiah kept pace right behind me as we headed up to the attic. At the top of the stairs I turned the light on and took a moment to look over at where Ophelia's body had lain in waiting not that long ago. A chill ran down my spine and I rubbed the goosebumps on my arms. The image steeled my resolve to get the things I needed and be successful. I *owed her* this.

The large gray trunk sat in just the spot I remembered. I lay my palm against the lock and uttered the word, springing the lock to open the lid. From the depths, I pulled a dark purple scarf and unwrapped our family's ritual athame. The only other time I saw it was when I read about it in our grimoire and searched it out.

It fit the bill precisely for the ritual. I ran my thumb over the nuummite blade. Its power sizzled against my skin. Nuummite is said to be one of the oldest of the earth's minerals. The stone itself will shield the bearer from negative energies, including curses and spells, while providing protection from black magic and evil deities. It occurred to me in that moment that I should have it in my possession at all times.

The purple cloth accompanying the dagger was on the list too, in a tangential way. According to the ritual instructions, the performer should be clothed in the attire of their ancestors. That cloak had been in my family for as many generations as had been written in the grimoires, so many of my ancestors wore it at one time or another.

The third item in the attic that made the list of being required for the ritual was five feathers from a leucistic peacock. A tall vase in the far corner held dozens of them, each in pristine white despite their time in the dust filled attic. Counting out seven, I gathered them in my fist, careful not to damage the tiny feathers.

"Carry these, please?" I handed them to Isaiah and returned the items we didn't need back to the trunk. "Let's go down to the attic and see if we can find the last item."

To be fair, I didn't know for certain if the item we

needed was down there, but I hoped we could find it in the sanctuary chamber. We needed a lotus bloom, fresh, not dead and dried. In many belief systems, the lotus symbolizes rebirth and resurrection. I remembered the well water supporting a number of blooms, but could remember if a lotus was among them.

As we traversed the stairs to the basement, an ominous rumble rolled through the house.

"Was that an earthquake?" I looked at Isaiah, eyebrows high.

"I think so, but not a natural one. We don't have earthquakes here."

"It seems that mother nature is trying to tell us that time is running out. We need to hurry."

Together we pushed the large armoire hiding the doorway aside, and I laid my hand against the rough hewn wood to open it. In the back corner, the well burbled. I took a moment to remove my shoes and socks out of respect to the goddess and the magic within. The instant both feet touched the soil, I left my physical body and felt air rushing past me. As I slowed and came to a stop, I had to bite my cheek to keep from losing my last meal.

"What the hell was that all about?"

"Apologies, my child. Our time grows short, and I have had trouble contacting you. Your natural defenses are strong and hold well against me in my weakened state."

"Goddess?"

"Yes, Leah."

"Is that why the evil spirit has been able to torment me less?"

"Partially. Although I believe she is biding her time and gathering her power."

"Why am I here?"

"Because I summoned you." Her tone suggested she disliked being questioned.

"Look, I appreciate you might be trying to help me, but I'm getting a little tired of being yanked around like a pawn in what seems to be boiling down to a war between you attempting to gain your freedom and my crazy-ass grandmother trying to steal your power."

Silence met my statement. For a second I thought I might find myself stuck here in the in-between since I'd made her angry. Instead, a heavy sigh echoed around me.

"You are not wrong. This war has been burbling since the day I was imprisoned here. Others have sought to drain my power and take it for themselves. This is the first time it has become a possibility that someone might be successful."

"So you need my help just as much as I need yours." I made it a statement and not a question because I didn't want her to dismiss me or try and pretend she had the upper hand.

Again, she took her time in responding to me. "Yes. I do. You re the first person I have ever even considered relying on. You have a natural-born power in addition to that which I granted you with the mark and the spirit magic you have chosen to embrace. They will all serve you well if you can learn to work them in harmony. They could tear you apart and cost you everything if you don't."

Wow. Heady stuff. Hearing an actual goddess tell you how powerful you have the capacity to be. Also, a little scary that she mentions that same power could destroy you. For the moment, my focus consisted of reuniting Ophelia's soul with her body and making sure my wicked witch of a grandmother could never, ever, hurt anyone again.

"Do you know where I can find the last item I need for the ritual? The bowl of all four elements? And is that a lotus back in the pool? If so, may I take it, please?"

"That is indeed a lotus blossom and you may have it for your spell. The bowl of the elements is an entirely different matter. As far as I know, one does not exist here in the sanctuary."

My heart sank to my feet at her words.

"However, you can create one. I can show you how."

Instead of telling me with words, the process played itself in my mind like a movie, complete with myself as the star. Step by step, she made sure I knew what to create with my physical self and how to apply my magic to end up with a vessel that would meet the requirements of the ceremony.

"Thank you for all your help."

I received no response other than a reverse of the process that brought me to her in the first place. The air rushed in the opposite direction and my stomach felt like it might fall out the soles of my feet rather than come up out of my throat. With a number of blinks, I found myself facing the well once more, the lotus blossom bumping up against the edge of the well as the bubbles pushed against it.

"Where have you been? You checked out on me."

"Sorry. The goddess apparently needed my attention." As I answered him, I walked over and checked the flower. "Can you get me a bowl or something so we can keep it in water for as long as possible? I'd hate to fail because the thing dried out on me and no longer qualified as fresh."

"Sure, be right back."

As his footsteps moved up the stairs, I took a minute to ground myself in the soil and the peace of the sanctuary. I let the tranquility climb my body and wash over me like a slow wave. It gave me a rejuvenation far better than sleep or food ever could. It topped off my magic and soothed my soul, preparing me for the rite I needed to perform the next day.

Isaiah returned, Tupperware in hand. "I thought with a lid we'd have less chance of spilling the water or having it get damaged."

"Smart." I winked at him and grinned.

"I do try."

Using the water from the well, I scooped the lotus blossom into the bowl and affixed the lid. Using a bit of magic, I placed two tiny air holes in the top. Even plants needed air to survive, didn't they?

"Thank you," I whispered as I turned around to

leave.

"You're welcome."

"I wasn't actually speaking to you, but I am thankful for your help too, so it's fine."

We left the small basement chamber and returned the armoire to its resting place against the wall. It could protect itself, but the less anyone or anything knew of its presence, the better. Back in the kitchen, we placed the collected items on the table and I looked at them thoughtfully.

One more thing and we would have her back with us. A thing that required my magic and skill to create. Hoping the goddess knew what she was talking about, I filled Isaiah in on what had happened while she had me away, wherever we'd been.

"The bowl doesn't exist."

He met my eyes. "It must. She could be wrong. She can't possibly know every single item on this peninsula. We-"

"Relax. As far as magical items go, I'm fairly certain she does know every single one in her territory. If she says it isn't here, then it isn't here."

"Then where do we find it?"

"If you would stop interrupting me, I could tell you

what she *did* say about it. Can I continue uninterrupted?"

He had the good grace to at least look a little sheepish. "Sorry. Carry on." He waved his hand at me, as if I needed the gesture to get the meaning of his words.

I made sure he could see me when I rolled my eyes. "I have to make the dish."

"You? Have to create an item needed for an ancient and powerful ritual?"

"Mmm. Oh ye of little faith. Yes, me. She showed me how and we can do it when we get back to the settlement at the east mountains."

"Then let's get back there and do this."

Before I could question the safety of leaving so late in the afternoon, another "earthquake" rolled through the house, stronger than the last. Dishes jumped around in the cupboards, and I heard pictures fall off the walls. If I hadn't grabbed the counter top for support, I would have landed on the floor, and Isaiah lost his balance, slamming his hip into the table.

"That can't be good."

CHAPTER SEVENTEEN

The windows rattled in their frames. Wooden boards creaked and groaned out on the porch. Outside the window, the trees were swaying across the clearing. Their movement made it clear the phenomenon encompassed more of the sanctuary than just the house.

"What is it? Do you think Rick feels it over by the mountain?"

Isaiah shook his head. "He says nothing is amiss over there. The pack doesn't feel anything either."

As the shaking ceased, the silence became

deafening. Neither of us made any move to set things to rights. The implications of the quakes frightened me. It took great power to upset the earth itself.

"I think we need to get back right away and get this ritual over with."

"Is it safe? Can we get there before it gets dark?"

Isaiah looked out the window and then checked the time on the stove. "If I hurry. But we don't have any time to waste. We need to leave now and hope we aren't waylaid."

"Let's do it." I finished packing what we needed into the backpack and we headed out the door.

At the edge of the clearing, I took a minute and increased the wards. Doing my best to include the area under the house and clearing as well, I asked the goddess to protect my home. Once I made my request, I climbed onto his back and we set off at a brisk pace. Within minutes, he reached top speed, and the trail flew by in a blur.

The sun dropped lower and lower as we traveled, making me worry we wouldn't get to the Eastern village in time. My senses remained extended to the woods around us, keeping a lookout for any others that might pose a threat. It remained eerily quiet. Nothing approached us, or even viewed us from afar, at least not that I could tell.

We didn't make it before dark, but we did make it uncontested. "That was too easy." I eyed the sky, looking for a threat.

"Agreed." Isaiah stood still, hands on hips and measuring his breaths to slow his heart rate.

Even for a wolf of his capabilities, the run was long, and he bore my entire weight, plus the backpack and its contents, for miles without stopping a single time. Rick ushered us into his cabin as I filled him in on what went on while we were at the house collecting the last of the items we needed.

"And the dish?" Rick knew before we left that we needed to find one.

"No. It doesn't exist. At least not here in the sanctuary. Or anywhere else the goddess has access to."

"You're sure?" His voice broke while asking the question.

"I'm sure. I spoke with her while in the chamber collecting the lotus blossom."

"What do we do now, then?" He sank into a chair, running a hand through his hair and leaving it sticking out in disarray.

Isaiah broke in. "Leah, don't torture him. You're a brat."

I gave him a half smile. "Fine." Turning to face Rick once more, I gave him a full smile. "Luckily, I can make one. It is, apparently, fairly difficult, but I have the requisite magic and components necessary."

"Do you think that you can make it quickly, or will it take some time?" He voiced one of my innermost fears.

The goddess said I could make one. She also said it took an infinite amount of skill and to get it right. If I didn't get it right, the ritual would fail. One chance. I had a single chance to create it and save Ophelia. Just one. No do-overs. No second chances. I'd never be able to "try again."

It took conscious effort to lower my shoulders from touching my earlobes and unclench my fists. My jaw ached from grinding my teeth, and I needed Botox to release the WTF lines between my eyes. To say I worried about my chances of doing it perfectly right the first time would be an understatement, but I couldn't show that to them.

"I have to do it. She said to sleep and rejuvenate tonight while I charge my crystals under the moon.

Tomorrow, when the sun is high, I can begin. It doesn't have to be high noon, but it must be created in the direct sunlight to balance the moonlight under which the ritual will be held."

"Then we better get you fed and put to bed, my dear."

We sat around the table and discussed plans. My gut clenched when Isaiah repeated that while there had been no more abductions, they'd also not found anyone who previously disappeared. Shelby's friendly face filled my mind. My heart stuttered.

Even though I knew, for a fact, that she would want me to take care of what I needed to do and not damn everyone by searching for her, it hurt. When I thought about how scared she must be, it got hard to breathe and I could barely keep my tears from falling. As soon as Ophelia came back to us we were going to find her. She and any of the others who disappeared and still needed rescuing. I would not abandon them.

"Le-ah... Yoohoo!" Isaiah's face hovered inches from mine. "We're losing you here. I think maybe you should consider going to bed now. Tomorrow is going to be an exhausting day for you and you need to get some rest."

Being told to go to bed like a child made me grumpy, but he wasn't wrong. Magic took a lot out of me and I needed every last bit of an advantage for tomorrow that I could get. My response as I stood? A long, drawn out yawn. I waved at the two of them and stumbled into the bedroom, landing face down on the bed. Jeans made okay pajamas, I guess, because that's what I had on and my pajamas lay too far away.

Nothing interrupted my sleep that night, which made me feel like something was up when I woke in the morning. The smell of coffee prodded me out of bed, and I found Rick on the couch with a steaming mug.

"I made plenty. Help yourself."

After doing exactly that, I returned to the couch and sat at the opposite end. For a while, we drank our caffeine in silence. Fog covered the clearing and we could hear the birds in the area but not see them. The muffled sounds brought me a semblance of peace.

"What if I fail?" My voice felt very small as I asked.

It took him a minute before he answered. "Everything we tackle in life has the possibility of failure. We cannot, as a species, be successful one hundred percent of the time. We feel the likelihood of failure more heavily when the action we are undertaking has a higher value weight in our life, but that does not actually increase the probability that you will fail."

"But what if I do? What if her soul is condemned to purgatory? What if everyone here in the sanctuary is tortured and killed by the evil spirit because I can't beat her?"

"Ah, Leah. Have you prepared the best you can? Done everything you know how to make it right? If you have, and I'm pretty sure that's the case, then all you can do is the best you can do and know that you tried. We can cross the other bridges when we come to them. Have faith. The thoughts you hold in your mind can and will affect the outcome of the situation."

My chin dropped to my chest. I didn't want to look him in the eyes and let him see my doubts. Letting my focus wanted out the window and back to my coffee cup, I took a deep breath. He had a point. Everything I'd done up to this point prepared me for what needed to be done. Yeah, I'd made mistakes. Screwed up big time, even. But I was going to give this everything in me and pray that it would be enough.

"You're right." Standing, I offered him a smile. "Thanks. I'm going to refill this cup and gather the supplies I need for the creation of the ritual dish. In case I need to do it more than once, I want to start as soon as the sun's rays reach the clearing."

He raised his cup to me. "Yell if you need any help. We'll be here."

As I doctored my coffee, I ran over the list the goddess had given me in my head. Plain old dirt, dug from the earth. Ashes from a wood fire. Clean, clear water from a source constantly in motion and creating bubbles of the air you breathe. Combine them into a clay, making sure not to work out the air bubbles trapped in the mixture. Dry in the flames of a fire burning by my magic alone.

On the surface, it sounded fairly straight forward. Somehow, I knew it wouldn't be. If the rite required this specific item, it must be more difficult than it seemed.

Not wanting to gather the water from the falls until I needed it, I collected and assembled everything else on an altar board I created from a stone slab in the cave. The sun was just peeking its way over the tops of the trees, giving me roughly half an hour before I could begin. Choosing to meditate for that time, I found a large tree and sat cross-legged at its base, situating myself among its roots and facing the fire pit where I'd be doing the work.

Eyes closed, I let my mind wander. My subconscious led the way for preparation of the tasks awaiting me later in the day. Consciously, I shut out the dark and negative. Only light and positive energy were allowed in my space. Deep breaths grounded me in calm. When the sunbeams hit me and warmed my face, I knew it was time and I was ready.

Every instrument to be used during the creation I chose with intention. The vessel used to carry water from the falls came from Ophelia's kitchen. I'd gathered the ashes from her own fireplace. The dirt I removed from the planter on her cabin porch. In every ingredient, I did my best to tie her to the process.

The others in the village knew I needed to be alone for the process and didn't interrupt, even after my cussing fit when the first two attempts were unsuccessful. Only Isaiah dared approach me when the third, fourth and fifth tries resulted in me chucking the useless, misshapen crock against a boulder and causing it to shatter.

"Leah."

"Not now!" I roared at him. "I only have time for one more try. Do not interrupt me."

Ignoring my outburst, he came and squatted beside me. Turning me to face him, he took my hands and planted a kiss on my forehead. Then, resting his nose against mine, he locked eyes with me and took deep breaths. In through his nose and blowing out gently against my lips. No words, just a calm example of what I needed right at that moment.

Following his lead, I let the frustration and anger drain away. He drew my focus back to where it needed to be. Not on the failures, but on the potential success of this next attempt.

He knew when he felt the tension leave me. My shoulders relaxed and I no longer gripped his hands in a bone-crunching hold. Even my heart rate slowed and steadied.

"Thank you." The whisper was barely more than a breath.

He nodded, smiled, and stood. After the first few failures, I'd needed more ingredients and the piles of newly gathered items sat in the sunshine, as if waiting for me.

Pulling the altar stone close, I said a brief prayer over it. Resting my palms against the ground I sat upon, I asked for grounding and guidance.

With sure fingers, I then took equal amounts of ash and earth and created a mound on the stone. Taking my time, I rounded out a small well in the center. Instead of pouring the water in straight from the container, I used my cupped hands to transfer it from the vessel. Then I mixed, kneading only until the substance would hold a form.

The bowl I manipulated into being was not large, nor fancy. But I made it with love and pure intentions. Centering it on the altar stone, I called forth fire from my magic, coaxing it to work with me instead of demanding it do my bidding. The clay that once was soft and soggy hardened to a sheen.

The imperfections in it were obvious. I made no attempt to hide them, for in all their glory, they made it what it was. They held it together, forged out of my love for Ophelia, not by my demand for an object needed for a purpose.

On the stone, it sat. Intact. Complete. And hopefully worthy of the task, I would ask of it later that night.

CHAPTER EIGHTEEN

Heads peeked out of doorways and from behind curtains as I gave a little whoop and did a little dance of excitement. Laughing at their attempts to see what was going on without disturbing me, I waved them all out.

"It's done. You can all come out now!"

I felt like a certain good witch telling all the little munchkins in the wizard's land that it was safe to leave their hiding places.

As they all joined me in the clearing, I held the object of my ministrations aloft. They looked at it, then at each other, and gave me a smile.

"I know. It doesn't look like much. But it will allow me to perform the ritual tonight, and that is all I care about at this point."

"I told you you could do it." Rick patted my shoulder.

Turning to Isaiah, I wrapped him in a hug. "Thank you. I don't think that last try would have been the one if you hadn't come out and helped me to find myself."

"Any time. I keep telling you, I will help you in any way I can. And for now, I suggest you let me make you some lunch so you can rest and relax before tonight."

"Always so bossy," I teased him.

The rest of the group began discussing lunch, and I listened in, appreciating each of them a little more for coming on this trip with me. All but one of them had known and liked Ophelia, so in addition to this being important to the sanctuary safety, they also wanted their friend back.

In the hours after creating the dish and needing to begin setting up for the spell, I ate and rested and meditated. Part of the time I spent sitting next to Ophelia's body in the guest room of Rick's cabin. In stasis, her face looked so serene and held none of the expression that always graced it in life.

"I will do this. I won't fail you, I promise."

Muttering the words over and over, I turned them into my mantra. I would not fail her. This had, over time, become less about needing her help to beat the evil spirit once and for all and more about knowing that she deserved my success. Nothing would get in the way of my rescuing her soul from wandering purgatory for eternity. Especially since I sent her there, and she did nothing to deserve it.

As the sun began to set, I prepared myself for the final time. This ritual gave me only a single, solitary chance at being successful. Everything I did, in every moment, needed to be focused. The spell and its instructions ingrained themselves in my brain.

My mental blocks to keep out the evil spirit worked so well that it left me feeling as if I was missing something. It seemed too quiet. Even with the explanation that this village sat in an area protected better than any other on the peninsula, it worried me that we saw no signs of her or any of the other intruders once we got here.

Taking the chalk I'd collected, I began to sketch the circle, and the runes described in the book. This part I wanted to complete in the daylight so I could clearly see if I made any mistakes. The entire sequence played through my mind as it had dozens of times since I first read them in the cave.

Rick and Isaiah helped me move her body into the circle so I could close it just before the sun disappeared. According to the book, she needed to be in place at sundown and wait there until the moon rose. Only then could I begin.

Stationed around the area were the other members of the team. They made up our security team and would hopefully prevent me from being interrupted in any way once the process began. Both the body and I needed to be protected until the ritual completed. After that, we could deal with whatever we needed to deal with.

Placing myself at her head, I sat down for one last meditation session. I opened myself up to the spirit magic fully, and at the same time asked the goddess' permission to use the magic of my mark as needed. Knowing that she needed me to be successful as well, I hoped she would look the other way and allow me to draw on its strength.

When the first beams of moonlight touched the edges of the circle, I stood. Moving counter clockwise, I placed the crystals and lit the candles while chanting the verse from the book. Reversing direction, I placed the other symbols and ingredients while singing the next verse softly.

As we moved further into the ritual, the wind whispered through the clearing, picking up my hair and tugging at it playfully. The flames on the candles rose higher, reaching for the sky. The sounds of the waterfall became both magnified and muted, clear as day but soft as a whisper.

Already my strength seeped out and less than half the ceremony was complete. Still, I moved on, unfaltering. I stopped for nothing. The dish I'd made of the four elements sat at Ophelia's head.

Chanting as the moon rose into the sky, I called her soul back into this world. Mist tangled with smoke and moonbeams, creating a shadowy figure. The vaguely humanoid shape hovered before me.

Raising my voice, I cried out to the heavens and asked for their blessings. Removing the athame from a thigh holster I'd found for it, I held it in my left hand and crouched over the elemental bowl. Drawing in a deep breath to give myself strength, I drove the blade through my right palm. Instructions had been clear that the blade must peek from both sides of the flesh.

The agony brought tears streaming down my face. Focusing on the pain, I let them flow, dripping off my chin and catching in the bowl below, mixing with my blood. As soon as the bowl filled, I moved it to set on her chest and began using the thumb of my left hand to painstakingly draw the required symbols on Ophelia's body.

My right hand had to be kept out at arm's length, as only the blood mixed with tears of physical suffering should be allowed to touch the body. Halfway through, I could no longer walk due to weakness. I crawled from her head to her toes, completing the bloody inscriptions. They covered her forehead, hands, abdomen and tops of her feet.

Blood loss stole my strength, impaired my vision and clouded my memory. I begged my crescent mark to renew me just enough that I might complete what I started.

The shadowy figure hovered directly above Ophelia's chest as I began the final chant. The howling of the wind and the roaring of the waterfall drowned out my words from even my own ears. Vague sounds made their way to me from outside the circle, but I couldn't afford to divert my attention from the task at hand. If an issue arose, I needed to trust that the others would do their part and take care of it.

With each word, the physical manifestation of her being sank back into her body. Kneeling at her side, I whispered the words over and over, repeating them even after my voice no longer worked right. My eyes slipped closed and still I mouthed the words. I didn't stop until I felt her chest rise beneath me.

Opening my eyes, I watched as her body drew another breath. At the fourth breath, I crawled to the candles and began extinguishing them in the order the instructions had indicated. Each time I chanted the closure phrase, which would bind her soul back to her body permanently, or at least until her true death.

By the time I had finished, she sat up in the circle, watching me. Dragging myself over to her, I offered up my right hand.

"You must remove it from me to complete the ritual. Then we will be done."

At first she just stared at my face, expressionless and eyes unblinking. She then lowered her gaze to the puddle of crimson droplets pooling beneath my outstretched hand. Rick held back Isaiah, who threatened to break the circle and remove it himself.

"Please." It took most of my strength to make the word loud enough to get her attention.

Pursing her lips, she reached out and grabbed the handle. The tiny movement of the blade had me screaming in pain. Fresh tears tracked down my cheeks. She hesitated.

"Just do it. One pull, straight out. Don't worry about me."

The seconds felt like hours. Finally, in a single swift arc, she yanked it up and out, raising her arm above her head. Yells broke out in the clearing around us, but I hurt too badly to see what created the commotion. The two of us remained in the circle, protected from whatever it was. That is until she grabbed my uninjured arm and used my hand to break it. Standing over me, she wielded the dagger at an unseen enemy as I let my eyes drift closed.

The sounds of the fight raging around me registered, but the ritual had taken everything out of me. My body refused to obey any command. That might have been because my brain turned to mush and couldn't issue a cohesive instruction to begin with.

Burning pain seared up my uninjured arm. It forced

my eyes open, clashing directly with the gaze of a dark-haired vampire who had his teeth sunk into my wrist. My attempt to pull away got me nowhere, and I watched in horror as he drank my blood down, Adam's apple bobbing with each swallow.

Bringing Ophelia back already took out more blood than I could stand to lose. If he continued, there would be nothing left, and I'd be drained dry. Every droplet leaving my body made me weaker and impaired my brain function even more. Someone else needed to help me, but I lacked the capacity to get their attention to do so.

Before I could gather the strength to cry out, the familiar black blade slammed into his temple. The sharp teeth retracted, and he fell to the ground. A newly resurrected Ophelia stood over me. In my head, the evil spirit began laughing.

Skirmishes waged all around me. The coppery tang of blood floated on the air, my own deterioration made it impossible to tell if the smell lingered from everything I used during the ceremony or if anyone else had a grave injury.

Fury coursed through me at the inability to defend my friends. Unable to defend even myself, I lay on the dirt, helpless. Useless. My vision blurred, making it hard to identify those around me. Bodies lay on the ground, but I couldn't see well enough to identify if they belonged to a friend or foe.

Before long, even sounds began to fade away, and I knew if I didn't get help soon I'd be in real trouble. Precious blood still dripped from both arms, weakening me further. Realizing my predicament, I began to make my peace with knowing I traded my life to give Ophelia back her soul.

While it broke my heart to know the others would have to face the evil spirit without my help, I'd done what I set out to do. Ophelia could help them. The goddess needed my evil grandmother defeated also, so she would probably help them. I hoped.

While the others engaged with the troupe of blood suckers someone else grabbed my wrists. Blinking to clear my vision, I saw Aaron above me. When did he arrive? Thankful to have someone else on my side, I relaxed, letting him drag me away from the fray. The pain jolted through my body and I let myself pass out.

CHAPTER NINETEEN

The cobwebs in my brain refused to let go. Every inch of my body thrummed with pain. Not even my eyelids wanted to move. This left me unable to see my surroundings, and I tried using my other senses to figure out where I was.

The surface I lay on definitely didn't feel like a bed or couch. In the air around me hung the cloying smell of damp dirt and decay. No light filtered through my eyelids, so either night had fallen or I'd wound up inside somewhere. No sounds reached my ears either. Where was I?

On my attempt to roll over and sit up my right arm jerked me to a stop, sending waves of unholy agony up the limb and into the rest of my body. For a second, I thought for sure my head would explode from the pain. Rolling back toward the offending limb, I got onto my side just quick enough to avoid vomiting all over myself. My last meal must have digested already because very little came out.

A breathy groan escaped me before I could stop it. Something told me I wasn't on friendly turf. Nobody I knew would chain me to whatever it was in the dirt. Panting, I lay still long enough to catch my breath and let the throbbing in my arm subside.

Digging deep, I searched my memories for how I ended up in my current predicament. My last clear thoughts were of performing the ritual to revive Ophelia. Had I been successful? My brain didn't want to connect the dots at that moment. Where were the others? In desperation, I tried calling to my magic in hopes of helping to heal myself enough to dampen the discomfort. Nothing but blank empty space answered me.

That tiny expenditure of effort did me in, and once

more I gave in to the blackness.

When I woke next, my eyelids were capable of moving and I blinked slowly, trying to focus my vision. No sunlight streamed in, nor any artificial light. As my eyes adjusted, I could slowly make out features of the room, none of which gave me a hint as to where I might be. It looked like a basement. Or a cave?

Pain rippled through me once more, eliciting another groan. Reaching out with my thoughts, I tried to contact Isaiah, but met nothing but blank air. Empty space. Squeezing my eyelids closed once more, I felt a tear squeak out from under one and slide down my cheek. Was he dead? He'd been with me throughout the ritual, and alive the last time I saw him.

Working backward frame by frame, like rewinding a movie in slow motion, I tried to put the missing pieces of my puzzle into place. Fuzzy and vague, many of them began coming back to me. My rite to return Ophelia's soul succeeded. I could remember the pain of her ripping the dagger from my palm. She also saved me from the bloodsucker that managed to gnaw on my arm.

Vampires! At the end of the ritual, vampires attacked us. The memory ignited my anger, and I clenched my teeth. Fury and worry fused together. Did the others survive? Where were they?

"Hello?"

Deciding it was an acceptable risk, I tried to call out, my voice rusty from disuse and my throat raw and scratchy. The only way someone could hear me would be if they sat inches from my mouth, and I could see far enough to know that nobody else was there.

Minding my right arm, by far the most painful of my injuries, I scooted and twisted until I could drag myself upright to rest against the rough stone wall. Pain drug me unconscious once more, but I was pretty sure it didn't last as long as the last two episodes. My stomach grumbled, a protest at being empty for way too long.

From my new vantage point, I could tell that I inhabited a small cave, possibly a cellar of some sort. Only the tiniest bit of light filtered in from somewhere far down a hallway or tunnel. If not for my wolf genes, I doubted I'd be able to see anything at all.

Closing my eyes once more, I tried reaching out to the goddess to beg for her help. My crescent mark still marred my flesh. I could rub my fingers over it in the darkness. But she either did not hear me or did not care to answer.

Leaning my head back against the stone, I cried

some more. Eventually, the tears ran out, and I simply sat there, waiting. For once I tried to sleep with the hopes that the dreamscape would appear and offer me an opportunity. Whether to escape, or simply to let someone know where I was, I just wanted contact with a friendly player. The game I found myself playing sucked, and I hated it more than ever before.

The dreamscape evaded me, but I dreamt of the skirmish after the ritual. Aaron! He had brought me here. Or had he? I only knew for certain he had begun to drag me away. After that, I had no way of knowing whether he, too, had been waylaid and perhaps overpowered.

All the pieces floated around in my mind, a brain soup of sorts. Each time I thought I had a lock on an explanation, someone's spoon stirred them all up again. Who else would want me here? Dear old Grannie wouldn't chain me to the wall. She probably would have killed me on the spot just to be done with it. My bet was on the vampires. Perhaps they wanted to keep me where they could drain my blood whenever they wanted.

Without my magic, I had no way to defend myself. They could come and go, feeding upon me whenever they wished, and I could do very little about it. If I continued to be so weak, lacking food and water to replenish myself, I might never be able to harness my magic again. It required a stronger vessel than I could offer it at the moment.

Time passed slowly. In and out of sleep I cycled, still hungry and thirsty and in immense pain. The dagger wound, which should have healed itself by that point, burned with an intensity that distracted me from the other, more minor, pains. I suspected an infection was settling in.

At some point, footsteps coming down the tunnel awakened me. Curling up into myself, I watched through slitted eyelids, fear almost paralyzing me. If someone had come to rescue me, they'd be calling my name.

A shadowy form entered the cavern, carrying a small lantern and a bag in the opposite hand. Without saying a word, I watched their approach.

"Leah?"

Blinking a number of times, I tried to focus in the onslaught of light. After being in the dark for so long, it made my head ache and my eyes burn.

"Who?" I couldn't force out any more than one single word.

"It's me. Aaron. I brought you some food and

water."

"A- Aaron? What am I doing here? I don't want food, I want out!" My raspy throat made the words hard to decipher in my own ears.

Instead of replying, he pressed a water bottle into my hands. "Drink it slow or you'll make yourself sick."

Deciding my thirst was a bigger priority than my anger for the moment, I drank. The second the first few sips hit my stomach, I had to fight to keep it down. Deep breaths and sheer willpower were all that kept me from losing it, just like he'd warned me.

The water soothed my throat some, making the words easier to get out. "Why am I here? Let me go. I thought you were my friend."

"I'm sorry, Leah. I can't let you out. She'll know. And she'll find you. And then you'll die."

"Who? Why can't I reach anyone else? Uncuff me!"

Yanking against the chain in my anger sent debilitating pain up my arm. I let the tears flow as I tried to reason with him. "Aaron. My hand is infected. If I don't get out of here, I'm going to die, anyway. A slow, painful death."

"Heal yourself." He seemed confused as to why I hadn't already done that.

"I'm trying to tell you. I can't. My magic isn't working. If it was, I wouldn't be stuck here still!"

"I'm sorry, Leah. I can't let you out. Not right now. I brought you food and some water. I'll try to come back soon."

He stood, and I grabbed at him with my good arm. I'd beg him if that's what it took to get me out of this hellhole.

"Please. Please don't leave me here. Where is Isaiah? And Rick? Do you know where Shelby is? Please Aaron." Tears fell harder with each word.

Pulling his arm from my weak grasp, he backed up a few steps. He looked down at me, his face clear in the lamplight. His skin looked pale, and he had large purple bags under his eyes. His hair hung stringy and limp against his forehead. His brows almost met in the center with his concentration focused on me and I could almost see him thinking.

"I'm sorry," he said again. "I can only fight her so much. You have to stay here for now."

He walked back up the tunnel without a backward glance, despite my pleas. I screamed his name, begging him to come back. The light extinguished, and I was completely alone once more. Alone, and cold.

Shivering, I curled up and cried. My hand hurt, to the exclusion of all other thought. Consciousness came and went. Hunger finally won out during one of my waking periods and I felt around for the bag Aaron had left. Emptying it, I found a couple of peanut butter sandwiches and some more bottled water.

Opening a sandwich, I ate half slowly, chewing deliberately. My stomach cramped at the introduction of food, but I knew I needed it to regain my strength. Despite my continued hunger, I stopped at the half and put the rest back in the bag. I didn't know when Aaron might return, and I needed it to last for a while.

In the dark and the silence, time ceased to make any sense. Crawling to the far end of the chain, my captivity forced me to relieve myself in the corner as far from where I sat as I could get. I finished off the sandwiches, but managed to make the water last a little longer. While my body still ached from sitting on the cold, hard surface, many of the other aches and pains had subsided, except the puncture wound in my palm.

That wound still hurt like no other. Eating the food went a long way to regaining some strength, but not enough to access my magic, if weakness was what kept me from it to begin with. If it was something else, I didn't know what to do. Aaron hadn't looked so good. If he died somehow, nobody else would know where I he kept me and I would slowly waste away.

Someone, someday, might find my skeleton while exploring and out of the way cave system, but they'd never know how I died or what I'd been doing down here. They'd be curious, I'm sure, about a body chained to the wall, but I doubted they'd ever uncover the truth.

On the other hand, nobody may ever find me, and this place would be my final resting place. My corpse would lie here, slowly decomposing in a cave where even mushrooms would probably never feed off my body. Maybe a few bugs would find their way, but then again, maybe not. Time would be the only thing to ravish my flesh until it, too, eventually gave up and left my bones in peace.

Morbid thoughts wandered in and out of my brain and I exerted no control over them. The delirium set in and took hold long before death would. Hungry and thirsty, I began to hallucinate.

At times I imagined my mother sitting next to me, sometimes holding my hand and brushing my hair back from my face.

Aunt Aimee paid me a visit, expressing how sorry

she was that we had missed out on so much together, telling me that if she had it to do over again, she would have taught me everything she knew from the very beginning, my mother's opinion be damned.

Other times I dreamed Shelby occupied a set of chains next to me. I cried to her and told her how sorry I was that I couldn't save her from her fate.

Even Isaiah's voice began echoing through my head. I couldn't see him like I could the others, but his voice was so real. He kept telling me to hold on.

"I'm just so tired now, Isaiah. I can't hold on anymore. I just want it to be over..."

CHAPTER TWENTY

"Leah. LEAH!"

His voice was so insistent, interrupting my peace and quiet when all I wanted was to sleep. Sleep helped to drown out the pain and the hunger. It muffled the sadness and the cold. In my dreams I didn't feel thirsty and my hand didn't hurt as badly as it did during my waking moments, which were thankfully getting to be fewer and farther between.

"Oh goddess. Leah. Honey, can you hear me?"

"Move aside. Let me see her. We need to get the

chains off." Ophelia's voice was a new one. Usually my imagination didn't include her.

The injury to my hand screamed awake at the jostling and I couldn't keep from crying out. Dehydrated as I may have been, there were still tears left in my eyes and they overflowed my closed lids.

"This is bad. This is very, very bad." Ophelia's voice again.

As much as I wanted to ask them what they were doing, my voice wouldn't work. Nothing wanted to work. The clanking of chains rang in my ears, louder than anything should ever have the right to be.

"We need to get her out of here. We need to take her someplace we can work on her." Isaiah made me laugh inside. Didn't he think if I could get out of here, I would have done that already?

"I'm going to put her out, or she won't even survive the move."

Ah, yes. Please, put me out. The suggestion sounded so good I tried to nod in agreement. I don't know if anyone saw me, or whether my head actually moved. Either way, blissful blackness took over.

Before I knew it, the darkness relinquished its hold on me. Light registered before anything else. If Aaron had finally showed up again, I'd kill him before I would let him leave me here again. Using both arms, I reached out and tried to grab hold of him, to hold him there, stuck like he left me.

Strong hands gripped my arms gently. "Shhh. It's okay. You're okay."

Tears fell again. The light, the soft surface, the warmth. Death had finally come for me. That had to be it. My eyes needed to open so I could see the angels. My lids felt like they weighed ten pounds, but determination to see my surroundings forced them open. Isaiah's face swam in front of me.

"Are you dead too?" He couldn't be. That's not what was supposed to happen.

"No, honey. I'm not dead. Neither are you."

"Are you sure? I was in this cave, and it was so cold. And I was so tired. And..."

"You're not dead, I promise. I'll admit it was a close call, but we found you."

"How? I couldn't use any of my magic, so I couldn't get free. I tried to call out to you, but I got nothing. I couldn't even connect with the goddess. Nobody answered me, no matter how hard I tried."

"We don't have a lot of answers right now."

"Where is Aaron? Have you seen him? This is all his fault."

Isaiah shook his head, rubbing his hand up and down my arm gently. My injured arm lay bandaged on the far side, away from the chance of being jostled. His response took a minute, and I could feel him arguing with himself about what to tell me.

"Aaron is dead."

Some part of me didn't want to believe it. The rest of me knew he told the truth. I'd been pretty sure he died when he didn't come back to bring me any more food or water. Despite chaining me to a wall in an out-of-the way cave, he didn't seem like he wanted to kill me. He seemed pretty sure his actions would save me from something.

"How?"

"Again, we don't know exactly. We're pretty sure the evil spirit killed him."

"Because he hid me?"

"Maybe."

Before I had a chance to ask any more questions, the door swung open and Ophelia poked her head through the crack. Her eyes locked on me and she stilled when our gazes met. Fear that she hated me now gripped me. My voice reverted to refusing to make words. I struggled to swallow.

Isaiah stood up. "I'll give you two a minute." He kissed my forehead. "I won't go far."

He nodded at Ophelia on his way out. She came over and took his space in the now vacant chair positioned beside the bed. For a minute, neither of us spoke.

"I'm so sorry."

The two of us spoke the same words at the same time. Still weak, I struggled to it up and face her, but couldn't manage to do it on my own. Instead of helping me, she laid her hand on my arm gently.

"Don't try to sit up. You need to save your strength. That was a very close call you just had. And you have nothing to be sorry about. Nothing at all."

"I almost stole your soul from you. All because I didn't want to lose you. I did what I did without even questioning whether you would be okay with it. I was selfish."

"You might have done it for some of the wrong reasons, but you did the right thing. I can't tell you how glad I am that I'm still here and I have another chance."

"But what if the ritual had failed? I almost couldn't

do it."

"No point in dabbling in the what-ifs now. It's done, and you were successful. We have bigger fish to fry, and not much time left."

"How long was I gone?"

She exhaled. "Nine days."

"Nine? Nine whole days?"

Nine days. My brain didn't want to accept that I lost nine days. That I spent nine days in the agony of hunger and pain. That Ophelia had been back with us for nine days and I hadn't gotten to spend any of them with her. That the evil in the sanctuary had had nine days to get the upper hand.

"How did you find me? I didn't think anyone would ever come for me."

She explained in short form what happened when I disappeared, what they did to try and find me originally, and how they finally managed it. She told me about finding Aaron's body, and I cried for him. She told me how Isaiah tried everything to find me. Everyone did. And then she told me that somehow the block between Isaiah and I broke, so he could feel me once more.

And they followed him right to me. Now, here we were.

Isaiah and Rick came into the room, Rick giving me a gentle hug. "Welcome back, kiddo. We missed you. You had us awfully worried."

The three of them looked at each other. Rick cleared his throat. "We need to get you back to the house, to the chamber in the basement. You will not heal if we don't. And if you can't heal, the evil spirit will win."

"Let's go then." Once more, I struggled to right myself.

Isaiah put out his hand. "Slow down there, turbo. You can't just jump out of bed. You almost died."

My gaze pinned him as I scowled. "I can get up." Intending to swing my legs over the side of the bed and prove him wrong, I stuttered when I found my legs wouldn't move at all. Nary a twitch in response to my brain's command. "What happened to me?" Panic set in. "Why can't I stand up?"

"Easy." Rick's voice was the voice of reason. "Your body has been through so much. On top of being starved, and cold. You had a terrible infection. Ophelia managed to halt the infection and give you enough strength that you woke, but you aren't out of the woods yet."

"Okay. Let's get back to the house, then."

"So." Isaiah took my hand. "You should know some other things that went on while you were missing. We killed the vampires. All of them."

"All of them?"

He nodded. "We're pretty sure anyways. We also found their hideout."

"Oh lord. Shelby? Did you find her? I dreamed of her while I was in that cave. It broke my heart all over again."

"Shelby is going to be fine eventually."

Tears of joy spilled over. My friend was going to live. As soon as possible, I planned to see her and tell her how sorry I was about everything.

"The evil spirit is angry. So angry. She'd planned on the vampires doing most of her dirty work for her, and the captives were their prize. We killed all her lackeys and took away her toys."

"Then I need to get healed and we need to kick her while she's down."

They spent the next few hours planning the move. I found out we ended up back in the East village after they found me because it was the closest safe place. Aaron hadn't actually taken me very far, and if someone had been walking in the woods when I could still scream, they might have heard me.

Isaiah came back in and sat next to the bed. I drifted in and out of sleep. Sometimes we would talk when I woke, sometimes I would just look over at him and smile. Ophelia needed to come back in and help me with the pain once the spell began to wear off. It reminded me just how bad of shape I really was in. She'd managed to mask most of it for me, between spells and potions, but it still lingered in my bones.

The group agreed to leave first thing in the morning to give me one more night of solid sleep before attempting to do the move. Rick made me small meals that I could only pick at, despite my hunger. By sundown, Ophelia came in to give me something to help me sleep.

"You'll heal faster if your body gets into a deep sleep."

"Thank you."

She smiled. "Once all this is over, we deserve a good, long vacation. To do nothing but sit on the beach and drink mimosas and eat chocolate-covered strawberries."

"Oh, that sounds so nice."

My eyes drifted shut and I never even heard her leave the room. For the first time since my ordeal began, the misty white fog of the dreamscape invaded my rest.

I heaved a sigh. "Please let it be the goddess and not the evil witch."

At least my pleas were heard.

"Child, we do not have long. Are you listening?"

"Of course I am. What other choice do I have?"

She snorted, very un-goddess-like. "Your body may be weakened, but your sarcasm is strong as ever. We will have one chance and one chance only to win this war. You need to get back to the chamber and heal your body and your magic."

"We go tomorrow."

"I have a plan."

She explained her idea down to the last detail. We bantered ideas back and forth, working out what I needed to do to be successful. Even at peak strength, my magic would be tested. Wrangling a spirit as powerful as my grandmother's made reuniting Ophelia's soul with her body look like child's play.

Fear that my body wouldn't be ready to withstand the pressure wound its way through me. Even if it hadn't just gone through a horrifically taxing ordeal, I would be asking a lot of it to manage this task.

"I will help you in any way I can. Once I am released from this oubliette, I will be at my full power and able to heal you in any way you need after the battle."

"As long as I'm not dead, right?"

"Well, yes. Even I cannot call someone back from the dead. But you seem to have a knack for avoiding death anyway."

"I'm trying, for crying out loud."

The mist began to fade. "We shall speak again when you are in the chamber and healing. Take great care."

Before I could reply, the dreamscape was gone, and I found myself staring at the bedroom ceiling. Pain wracked my body. The trek to the house would not be pleasant.

CHAPTER TWENTY-ONE

The argument over whether I would walk, be carried, or ride in the stretcher that originally brought Ophelia to the village ended abruptly when "a" I couldn't even stand up and "b" I could barely tolerate Isaiah's touch even after the pain blocking spell. Stretcher it would be. As much as I despised being carried along like an invalid, I had no other choices and we couldn't hang out and wait for me to get any better.

From the bed I shouted requests as they rounded up the last of our things to take back. Did they get my backpack? I wanted to bring the elemental dish home with me. Where was it? What happened to my family's athame? That, I wanted to hold in the stretcher with me. The protection it provided would help my weakened self immensely if we ran into trouble.

At some point, I dozed off again, waking only when they came in to transfer me to the stretcher. We'd lost one of our group to the vampire attacks the night of the ritual, and I'd missed the funeral the next the day. It left us one warrior short, but Ophelia and her magic would help if needed.

The move from the bed involved more pain and more than a few tears, even with Ophelia helping by magic. Panting, I lay for a moment with my eyes squeezed closed before I signaled they could go ahead and move me. Once the stretcher got lifted and they maneuvered it out of the house, the jostling lessened.

Ophelia leaned over me. "I can send you to sleep for the duration, if you prefer?"

Wincing at a slight jolt, I declined. "Thanks, but not yet. I feel like I've been asleep forever already. If it gets too bad, though, I might change my mind."

"Just let me know."

Along the path, we discovered evidence of more

earthquakes like we felt at the house, even though there had been no shaking in the village. Trees lay across the path in a few areas, uprooted completely. In other places, cracks in the earth crisscrossed the path, some only a couple inches deep and some a foot or more.

Many of the animals that inhabited the woods remained quiet that morning. A few calls could be heard in the distance, but we didn't see another living thing outside of our group. The silence made me aware of every sound. Each individual's breath, the beat of their footsteps, registered in my ears.

Rick and Isaiah chatted quietly at the back of the group, protecting our rear. Their voices carried to me, but I couldn't make out the words, perhaps due to the headache and the ringing in my ears that started suddenly. Just moments before, my hearing had been perfect in the silence. That addition to my laundry list of ailments was less than pleasant.

An hour into the walk, perhaps slightly more, the group suddenly came to a stop. Thanks to all my pain, I couldn't sit up or wrangle myself into a position to see the problem. Rick and Isaiah both moved past me to inspect the hold up.

"What's going on? Is there a problem?"

Ophelia came to stand next to me. "One of the earthquakes creates a fissure across the path. It connects to the stream, so the water has been rerouted. From here it looks to be fairly deep, so they are surmising the best route to take around it."

Rick raised his voice. "We're gonna take a little break here, have a snack and rest while we figure out how best to cross this new obstacle."

The ringing in my ears reached a crescendo and then suddenly silenced. Every last sound became crystal clear once more. Odd, but not unexpected in my current condition, I supposed.

The guys carrying my stretcher laid it gently on the ground at the base of a humongous oak tree I'd never seen before. The small pillow supporting my head gave me a slight visual of something other than the sky, but stiff muscles prevented me from looking around when what I really wanted to do was get up and see the stream for myself.

Isaiah came to kneel next to me. "Do you need a drink? I can help you sit up."

"Yeah, thanks. And I really want to be able to look around. Ignore me if I make any sounds. I already know it's going to hurt, but I've decided it's worth it."

He grimaced, but nodded his agreement. Slipping one arm beneath my neck and shoulders, he gave me the opposite hand to hold on to and lifted me into a sitting position. He slipped around behind me and nestled me into his lap so I could lean against him. The pain had me gasping, but I got the view I wanted. Sure enough, a wide new stream bisected the path we needed to cross.

Once I got settled and the worst of the new pain subsided, he gave me a water bottle. "Here, are you hungry?"

"Just water for now, thanks."

Rick came back to join us. "We are going to find an appropriately sized tree to fell and use as a bridge. The water is too deep to risk crossing without a bridge of some sort and even the original stream is too dangerous to use as a work-around."

Resting against Isaiah, I felt a small tremble in the earth beneath me. "Did anyone else feel that?"

Head shakes all around. Even Isaiah and Rick, right next to me, felt nothing. Maybe all I felt was a tremor in my body, not the ground. I watched as two of the guys wandered off to find a tree, followed by Ophelia, to help with the taking down.

Ringing began to buzz softly in my ears once more,

making focusing on the conversation difficult. With my eyes closed, I attempted to use my magic to feel the area around me, but got little more than a sense of confusion. It wasn't clear whether the confusion dwelled in my head or my surroundings.

Another tremor ran through me, this one more intense than the last. Before asking, I looked around and nobody else seemed to have noticed it. Rick caught my scowl and looked around.

"Are you okay?"

"Something isn't right? Like, I keep feeling trembling and I could swear it's coming from the ground, but none of you seem to notice. My ears are ringing and I just don't feel right."

Nearby, a tree came crashing to the ground.

"We'll be out of here soon enough. Part of it could be you feel a little helpless, which is an uncomfortable situation to be in."

Isaiah tightened his arm around me lightly, meant to be reassuring, but I gasped at the pain.

"Sorry."

"I'm fine. And Rick's probably right."

As they got the tree in place, Isaiah helped me get resettled on the stretcher and Ophelia gave me another dose of a pain blocking potion.

"We're about at the limit of what I can help you with unless you go to sleep. Sorry."

"I'll make it. Thank you for everything."

Just as they got the stretcher in the air, another tremor ripped through the ground, causing everyone to stumble a little bit.

"Nobody can tell me they didn't feel *that*!"

"We need to get going!" Rick yelled at everyone and the group headed for our tree bridge, en masse.

The ground bucked under their feet, throwing everyone off balance.

"Go, go, go!"

The sky darkened, and the water in the stream began to froth and bubble beneath the log. The dirt vibrated. Even the temperature began to drop.

Rick led the guys carrying the stretcher onto the log and Isaiah followed closely behind. Ophelia stood on the far side, using her powers to try and hold the log steady for us to cross. Underneath her, the path jumped, and she fell to the side, losing concentration. The log began to roll and twist.

Rick jumped and landed on the opposite shore. Just as the front of the stretcher made it all the makeshift bridge, the log rose straight up and turned sideways. Isaiah, the guy holding the back of the stretcher and I plummeted into the icy water.

Sinking, I used every ounce of strength I could muster to force my useless legs to kick. I needed air. The pain made the effort excruciating, but I made it to the surface in time to drag in a breath before falling beneath the surface again.

Of the three of us who fell into the water, I couldn't locate either of the guys. Knowing Isaiah, he had to be severely injured or otherwise engaged to not be helping me. My blood pounded in my ears, mixing with the god-awful ringing. Stars burst against my eyelids. Kicking harder, I tried to get to the surface again for more air. If I didn't take a breath soon, I would pass out and drown. Why did death have such a hard on for me lately?

Something hard and unyielding caught my arm as I reached for the surface and I grabbed onto it, trying to leverage it to get above the waterline. Pulling my head above the waves, I took a deep breath, followed by a couple more. When I had enough oxygen to begin to clear my head, I tried looking around for the others.

Without help, I couldn't get out of the creek, and if I didn't get to dry land, my muscles would give out, and

I'd be back to fighting the current for the right to live. If I'd thought my body hurt before, everything was on fire now. All the water in my eyes made my vision blurry, and it burned just to open them.

The ringing in my ears subsided some, but I still couldn't hear anything around me.

"Isaiah? Rick? Ophelia?"

Nobody answered my call. I didn't recognize the area I surfaced in and didn't have any clue how far down the river I'd been swept by the current. Trying with everything I had to pull myself onto the bank just made me weaker. Chilled by the freezing water, I began trembling so hard my grip on the branch kept slipping.

"Help me, please!"

My voice didn't reach very far, but I also reached out to Isaiah mentally. Nothing. Please don't let him be dead. My connection to the goddess was also silent. My injured hand was so weak it couldn't be used for hanging onto the branch anyway, so I reached out and shoved it into the earth along the bank.

"Please," I chattered, my teeth clanking together and making me stutter, "please get me out of here. Just out of the water before I drown."

Stillness met my request. Tears mingled with water

dripping out of my hair. Throwing my head, I looked to the sky and begged one last time. I just needed to get on solid ground, nothing more for the moment.

Instead, I began making my peace with the situation. I would hold on as long as I possibly could, but eventually I would grow too weak. Even with my arm wedge in as far as I could get it, as soon as I lost consciousness or lost the strength I would be washed downstream and pulled under. My hope was that I'd already be unconscious and wouldn't be aware that I was drowning. The thought of drowning terrified me.

Time passed slowly. Eventually, I could only keep my nose and mouth out of the water if I tilted my head all the way back. Desperation brought me an idea.

Using the roughness of the branch and the small protrusions, I tore open the wound in my hand, scraping off the scab. Fresh fire roared up my arm, making me lose track of my plan for a minute. Blood flowed. Pressing my palm up against the branch, which I prayed might instead be a root, I fed it my life force.

"Here, take it. I give it to you and all I ask in return is help out of this fucking stream!"

My hoarse voice made the words difficult to understand, but I knew the earth could feel my intentions. The blood that didn't get absorbed ran down my arm, the only feeling of warmth I felt like I'd had in ages, until it hit the water's surface.

A load groan sounded from somewhere nearby. As it registered, I realized the ringing in my ears had subsided at some point. With a creak and a rumble, the root, and I'm so thankful it wasn't just a branch, drug my wet carcass up out of the stream and left me laying face first in the pine needles and dirt. Once more, I found myself crying, this time with tears of joy.

My current situation might suck; I was cold and wet and in oh so much pain, but I wasn't going to drown. I'd been given another chance.

Before I had a chance to think of my next steps, I felt myself lifted into the air, blue light surrounding me. My body slammed back onto the dirt with my face toward the sky, knocking the wind out of my lungs. As I tried to draw the air back in and erase the stars from my vision, an eerie figure leaned over me.

"Girl, why won't you just be a good girl and die, like your auntie and your momma did?"

CHAPTER TWENTY-TWO

Still lacking the air to breathe, much less respond, I stared at the spirit in shock. My chest heaved as I struggled to make the muscles relax enough to begin taking breaths again. My body felt frozen to the dirt. Even if I wanted to get up and flee, I couldn't. Not that it would have done me any good.

Fear coiled through me. I'd been worried about our confrontation, expecting to meet her at the top of my form. Being injured and mostly cut off from my magic made the meeting terrifying. My plans had included having Ophelia and the others at my side, and she managed to get me alone, injured, and practically helpless.

At long last, my diaphragm released, and I drew in a deep, shuddering breath. "Why? Why do you hate me so much? What have I ever done to you?" I whispered the words.

The specter laughed in my face. "You have

absolutely no idea. Your mother almost avoided death by keeping you in the dark, but the she decided to share everything she knew with you. Well, almost. Some things made it to her grave, which pleases me greatly. So. If you really must know what you did to me, I'll tell you."

Unable to get up, I tried to follow her figure as she glided around me. Much like a teacher giving a lesson might pace the classroom to check on their students. Pain wracked my body as I tried to gather magic, pleading once more for the earth to assist me.

"It's quite simple, really. You were born with the magic I deserved and I want it. Somehow, the fates decided that you, of all people, were worthy." She sneered. "Imagine that?"

Her magic ripped at me, pulling me upright and dangling me so that my toes just touched the dirt. Pain darted down my extremities and I bit my cheek to keep from crying out; I refused to give her the satisfaction. She came to hover directly in front of me.

"Your mother robbed you of so much, child. Your birthright could have made you so much, but look at you now. She hid it from you and you are *pathetic*. Absolutely an embarrassment to our line."

"What are you talking about?" The words came out as more of a squeak than I'd intended. I wanted to show her she didn't scare me, but my condition made it difficult to pretend.

"Everyone tried so hard to help you. Aimee left you all the secrets, and for a while I was afraid I wouldn't get them away from you before you learned too much. Thank goodness Aaron was such a good little slave. At first."

She glared at me, flinging her hands out and causing rocks and branches to swirl around us in a mini tornado, expressing her displeasure. Pebbles stung my face and the bare arms I couldn't raise to protect myself. Blood trickled warmly down my temple from a particularly sharp rock.

"Even while under my full control, he managed to drag you away and hide you somewhere I couldn't find you. Despite the torture I inflicted on him, he never told me where you were. I won't bore you with the details, but suffice to say I tore him to pieces, and he still protected you. Apparently his guilty conscious over killing your mother and stealing the grimoires was stronger than the pain. I almost hated to lose him, but no bother. I don't need him now. Your friends were kind enough to bring you right to me."

Despair stole my breath once more. Poor Aaron. My instincts had been right. He wasn't a bad guy. Even until his death, he tried to help me. Tears threatened, but I swallowed them down. We would find his remains and give him a proper sendoff. If I survived this.

"So many secrets, so little time. Do you know who your father is, young lady? Did your mother share that with you? Give you any hints at what lies in your DNA? The vampires, useless though they proved to be, wanted your blood so badly." She laughed in my face.

"I don't think who my father is matters at this point, do you?"

Breathing took up a good portion of my concentration, making my conversational skills less than stellar. My only goal for that moment was to buy myself some time, hoping the others would find me. Or my connection to the goddess opened up once more. Anything that could help me get myself out of her clutches, even if I meant running away and fighting another day. My pride already hit rock bottom. I'd scurry away like a scared bunny rabbit from a fox, given the opportunity.

"Ah, but it could have saved your life. I don't

suppose it would hurt anything to tell you at this point. You can take the information to your grave, just like your mother did. You are the last of the line now, and it will not continue." She paused. "Well, do you want to know or not?"

Attempting to keep my head in the game, knowing if I got out of this mess the information could help me, I tried my best to be nonchalant.

"Whatever. Like you said, knowing won't help me now." Some of the strength crept back into my tone, even if only as a loud whisper.

She laughed. "I can see the curiosity in your eyes. You're dying to know. And I'm going to tell you, just for the fun of it. Because I'd like to see your face when you learn what your mother hid from you all those years. What you missed out on, thanks to her. And, you know, Aimee knew as well and never breathed a word of it to you." She paused, for dramatic effect most likely, and then spit out the words as if they tasted bad.

"You are the only living, for now, direct descendant of Fenrir. How the wolf managed to father a child to continue his line is beyond me, but he did. The story was nothing more than a legend for so many years, yet here you are. He existed and took a liking to your mother, of all people. I had to kill him too, which took quite a bit of effort. I'll have you know."

Surprise stole my words. Descendant of a demi-god. My Norse history was admittedly lacking, but wow. Okay then. My brain began to work furiously. This information explained my somewhat terse relationship with the goddess of the sanctuary. She didn't smite me for my attitude toward her because perhaps she couldn't? We existed on similar power levels. I just needed to learn to access mine.

Questions swirled in brain, temporarily making me forget my current situation. That is, until she used her power to restrict my breathing. The pressure on my throat brought immediate stars to my eyes. Just enough air got in to keep me conscious.

"Now, now. Don't go thinking this information will save you. If you haven't got it yet, you won't. I am aware at our pitiful attempt to access your wolf. Couldn't even do it without help."

Shifting wouldn't help me now, unless it brought healing to the ridiculous amount of pain I was in, but more magic was in me somewhere. If I could use it, I had a chance.

Pain rocked me as the hole in my hand opened

wider. The blood ran, dripping down my fingers and into the dirt below. This time, I couldn't swallow back the tears.

"You know," she continued in a conversational tone, "that because of the way his power has passed on to you, the only way to kill you is to bleed you dry first? Because the magic runs in your veins. I have to remove it all before I can do away with your body in the normal way. Killing your father taught me that lesson. It took a good bit of trial and error to figure it out."

Slashes opened up along my forearms, more blood trickling out. They burned in a whole new way. And yet, something crept into my awareness that hadn't been there before. A presence. Closing my eyes for a second, I considered that it might be Death himself come to collect me.

A stinging wracked my abdomen, and I knew without looking I'd begun to bleed there too. My brain began getting fuzzy, and I knew blood loss factored into the feeling. I didn't have much time. Gathering what little magic I had in me, I called out for help once more. I offered up my lifeblood for the chance to bring her down.

At that point, I knew I'd sacrifice myself if I could

take her with me. Eyes still closed, I pushed all the magic left in me out into the universe. Her shriek sent my eyes flying open.

Then laid open beneath her, a crystal-looking box revealed. The blue light surrounding her pulsed as she attempted to move away, but she appeared to be held tight.

At either side of me, I felt someone gently take my hands, holding loosely to my wrists.

"Mom! Aunt Aimee!" They gave me sad smiles, but sent me warmth and love through our bonds.

Without their support, I would have crumpled to the ground, as my grandmother's attention turned fully committed to extracting herself from her position of what I assumed to be the oubliette the goddess had referenced. She almost made it, having over half her body back over solid ground and pulling herself slowly along.

At her head, the apparition of an enormous silver wolf appeared. I stared in wonder. Could it be?

The jaws of the wolf opened wide, crushing down on the phantom arm of the spirit, eliciting an ear-splitting scream from her. The wolf did not move, holding her in place.

The goddess' voice rang out. "You, Leah, must do the rest. She must be forced into the prison by you alone. I will try to help you so that we may trade places and she will be caught here forever."

Weak from blood loss, I struggled to move forward. My mom and Aimee basically carried me.

"We can no longer interfere with magic, but we can assist you in any way physically. I have slowed the bleeding, and we can get you to her, but you must do the rest." Each of them planted a kiss on my cheeks.

Using every last vestige of my strength, I pulled my magic around me. The wolf never took his eyes off me as I approached. My mother and Aimee released me and moved back. Somehow, I made my arms obey as I drug the evil soul back over the crystal cage. Kneeling, I positioned myself over her, both hands flat against her as I held her down. She struggled, opening bloody slices along my skin, but still, I refused to stop.

With a push, both physical and metaphysical, I shoved her down. The goddess continued to yell at me to reach in and pull her out, but I ignored her. Her white light began to shine so brightly that my vision was occluded. An instant later, I could no longer feel the presence of my grandmother's ghost or the goddess. The bright white light winked out of existence. As I collapsed, my face hit dirt instead of the smooth, clear-ish crystal I'd just been looking down on. Silence fell.

I felt Aimee and my mom pull me into a sitting position. My mom placed herself in front of me and looked me directly in the eyes.

"Leah Catherine, I am so very sorry." She reached up and wiped away the blood and tears from my face.

Aimee grasped my hand. "We both are. I am so, so sorry."

"Don't be sorry. It's over now. I miss you both so much." I tried to hang on to them as they began to fade before my eyes. "It is really over now, isn't it?"

Stepping closer, the wolf figure interrupted. "She is contained, and it is unlikely she will ever escape. If the oubliette can imprison a goddess for millennia, it is probably capable of containing a witch. However, never let your guard completely down. If they decided to work together, the results could be unexpected."

My eyes stayed trained on him. "Are you my father?" I had to know.

He shook his shaggy head. "Not your father, child. I am sorry. She managed to extinguish him completely with the ritual she used to kill him. But I am, indeed, your ancestor. I must go, but we are connected now and I will return. I have much to share with you in the future."

With those words, he faded from sight, leaving me with no opportunity to ask any other questions. Turning to my mother and Aimee, I begged them to stay.

"Please, don't go. Don't leave me."

"We have no choice." My mother looked heartbroken. "We have led your friends this way and they will be here soon."

Aimee stroked my cheek. "We have stopped the bleeding. You will be fine. It might take some time, but you will be good as new."

"I need you guys. Can you please stay with me? Please."

Tears coursed down my cheeks. I'd cried more in the last few days than the rest of my life combined. I might not bleed out, but soon I would turn into a desiccated husk if I kept up with the waterworks.

Both of them shook their heads in sorrow. My mom leaned in and kissed my cheek. "It is time. Our souls have lingered here longer than usual already. We managed to stay because we knew you would need us, but our time here is coming to an end. I love you so much, my darling, and I hope you can forgive me for everything I cost you."

"Already forgiven." My sobs made it hard to get the words out. "I love you."

Aimee took her turn to kiss my forehead. "I love you, Leah. Always have. And I, too, owe you an apology for all the secrets."

By this point, I could only shake my head. It was like I was losing them all over again. Emotional aches hurt so much more than the physical ones.

Aimee squeezed my uninjured hand. "Listen well, Leah. Go forward with love. You have much to learn, but you have so much potential. The house and this sanctuary are full of secrets. You have discovered a few of them in the grand scheme of things. I left you hints everywhere. Be looking for them and pay attention to the little things. They lead to the much bigger ones."

"Leah!"

Shouts could be heard in the distance, getting closer rapidly. Isaiah and the group found me and were almost there.

The spirits of my mom and aunt stood and looked down upon me. No more than iridescent shimmers in my field of view at that point. I heard their voices one last time.

"I love you, Leah."

With those final words, they were gone. Footsteps crashed through the brush as Isaiah burst into the clearing. Dropping to his knees beside me, he gathered me in his arms. With a wan smile, I leaned my head up against his chest and let out a sigh. This time, I could close my eyes and relax. For now, the threat was no longer.

CHAPTER TWENTY-THREE

Sunlight streamed through the window and danced across my closed eyelids. My breath moved easily in and out of my lungs, tender and sore but not outright painful. After taking stock of my ailments and injuries and finding them not to be life threatening, I finally opened my eyes.

The ceiling above me looked just like a remembered it. Turning my head to the side with great care, I saw all the same things I'd left in my bedroom before. Next to the bed sat the unoccupied arm chair usually found in the corner. Voices filtered down the hall, probably from the kitchen. Did I call out to them, or attempt to get myself out of bed on my own?

Testing my limbs and their willingness to cooperate with my commands, I shifted my legs up and down. When they obeyed, I swung them over the side of the bed. Using my uninjured hand, I pushed myself into a sitting position and held myself reasonably steady. The room spun for a minute, but subsided after a few blinks and deep breaths.

Before I gathered enough strength to attempt standing, I heard footsteps coming down the hall in my direction. The door pushed open and Isaiah stuck his head in, Ophelia and Rick right on his heels.

"Don't even think about it. You may be feeling better, but the last thing we want is for you to fall and knock yourself in the head. You'd end up right back where you were."

Instead of being mad, I just laughed. I'd totally take being told what to do if it meant not being dead. The laughter hurt my ribs but didn't bring agony.

"Hey there, you guys."

The three of them stood in front of me. I could feel them inspecting me individually. Ophelia put out her hand. I felt her magic ash over me, probing and searching for injuries or illness. The infection in my hand had disappeared, even though the wound still needed time to heal. Unsure of how long I'd been out this time, I knew it had been a while because of how much better I felt.

They began to pepper me with questions all at the same time. Ignoring them, I held up my hand.

"I'm happy to feel you in, but I need to pee, and I am starving."

They jumped to action. Rick headed to the kitchen, offering to get food ready. Isaiah and Ophelia positioned themselves to help me stand and make my way to the bathroom. Once I'd taken care of the necessities, I stood in front of the mirror and stared at myself. Outwardly, my hair was a tangled rat's nest and my skin pale. The bags under my eyes would have garnered overweight fees at any airport.

But I wasn't dead. She hadn't bled me dry. With the help of my loved ones, I'd won. And boy, did they leave me some baggage to unpack.

Using the wall to steady myself, I opened the door and made my way down the hallway. Isaiah jumped up and held his hand out, helping me to get from the wall to the chair. Rick sat a plate of food in front of me and they all sat and watched me expectantly.

About five bites into the meal, I could tell they were maintaining their patience by only the barest of threads. Smiling, I invited them to ask their questions.

"What do you guys want to know first?"

"Is she gone?"

"How did you do it?"

"Was that really your mom and Aimee?"

Their inquiries tumbled over one another, making it hard to separate the individual voices, and I laughed at them without answering. Continuing to take bites, I waited for them to stop chattering. At long last they quieted, and I told my story.

Everything I remembered from the minute I ended up dumped in the creek until they found me at the clearing in the forest was relayed between bites. Some of my recollections stayed fuzzy in my mind, and no matter how hard I tried, I could not clear them up.

The three of them exclaimed over who my father had been revealed to be, and posited questions about who the wolf that visited may have been. We pooled our ideas about the meaning of Aimee's last message. For a minute we voiced concerns that the goddess might be out for blood since I had not released her from the oubliette like she'd demanded.

"If it comes up, I'm just going to tell her it took all my strength to get the evil spirit in, and I collapsed right after. I had nothing left to get her out. Hopefully she'll be tied up for a while with her new roomie anyways."

We sat at the table and talked as the sun crossed over the sky. At one point, I looked out the window to see a familiar face crossing the clearing. Jumping up with joy, I winced and braced myself against the table and waited for her to let herself in before I released the support and threw my arms around her.

"Shelby. Oh my gosh, Shelby..."

Once more the waterworks opened and I cried. This time, at least, they were tears of joy. She cried too. We held each other close, both of us grateful to see the other amongst the living. So many had been lost in this war.

"You did it? It's really over?" Shelby's voice quivered as she asked.

I nodded my head against her shoulder. "I have so much to tell you for it to make any sense at all, but we don't have to worry about her for a long, long time. Maybe never."

"That's all that matters right now."

Others filed through the kitchen throughout the day to see how I was doing, to say thank you, and to verify that, for now, they were safe. Much still needed to be figured out, but for the time being, we all just wanted to let our guard down and rest.

Rick and Ophelia bade us goodbye as the sun went down, making plans to return the next morning. Isaiah and I moved to the couch in the living room, staring at the flames in the fireplace.

"Everything feels so surreal right now."

The words to explain how I felt inside wouldn't come. At least, not any of that made sense. Since the day I got the cryptic voicemail from my mom, I'd been stretched thin and constantly on guard. So much had changed. Incredible things had been gained, tempered by devastating loss. Life would carry on so much differently than just a few short months ago.

"One day at a time. We have the rest of forever to figure it out, right?"

Scooting closer, I entwined my fingers with his and leaned against him. "That sounds nice. The rest of forever."

ABOUT THE AUTHOR

Tera Lyn Cortez made the leap from voracious reader to author in 2019. In addition to books of every kind, she is a lover of coffee, the ocean, and all things chocolate.

Her home life consists of being a wife and mother to five in the lovely Pacific Northwest, although she admits to being consumed with Wanderlust. Life as a writer allows her to indulge in traveling both our world and those that live only in our imagination when she can't leave her office.

http://www.teralyncortez.com/

http://www.facebook.com/teralyncortez

ACKNOWLEDGMENTS

So many people go into the making of a book that it can be hard to keep track. In addition to my friends and family who encourage me when I'm feeling overwhelmed, I've got the professionals in my corner helping me make these books the best they can be before I send them out into the world.

Thank you to Amanda, my editor at Dark Raven Edits, for helping to whip the story into shape and making sure that we get rid of as many of those pesky typos as we can. (I know I always make plenty!)

Do you love this cover? I certainly do! Thank you to Melony at Paradise Cover Design for creating exactly what I wanted, even though I didn't know what I wanted at the time!

YOU ARE ALL AMAZING!